THE MARINES

The Return of the Marines

Book 3

Colonel Jonathan P. Brazee

USMCR (Ret)

The Marines

Copyright © 2012 Jonathan P. Brazee

Acknowledgements:

I want to thank all those who took the time to pre-read this book, catching my mistakes in both content and typing. From VFW Post 951 in Bangkok, I need to thank Ricky Reece, MacAlan Thompson, Al Fleming, and Bill Bernstrom for their proofreading and fact-checking. I need to thank Ann Bunch, a reader who has left reviews on my other books and gave me pre-publication comments on this one. And of course, my editor, H. Ray, who helped me polish this manuscript.

Printed in the United States of America

Semper Fi Press

Pete slowly pushed forward along the path, senses on high alert. It sounded like if there even were Chinese soldiers on that helo, they had been inserted only a short distance away. If they were there, he didn't know what their mission was, which way they were going, or how many there were. On the plus side, they probably wouldn't be expecting anyone to be out here in the middle of the jungle, a good 500 meters from the northern shoreline.

He looked back along the path. He was probably only 30 meters from where he had left Analiza and the others, but it felt like he was completely alone. He knew he should get back, or at least wait for the rest of his team, but he wanted to get just a bit further in order to see if in fact there was anyone in their path.

Stepping carefully, he moved forward another 10 meters to where a dense stand of some sort of tall, bamboo-like grass formed a barrier just off the path. Although it was only about a dozen feet high or so, it was a good four feet wide and so tightly packed as to act as sort of a pseudo-tree trunk. He had no idea what would cause it to grow that way, but it would give him some cover from which he could try and see if there was anyone in front of them.

In back of him, he could hear nothing. His charges were either silent or the jungle too dense for sound to travel far. In front of him was also silent. Even the sounds of explosions off in the distance seemed muted in the humid, oppressive heat.

He really should not be alone, and he knew he needed to get back. But first, he wanted to look down the path to see if there was any sign of the Chinese. He pulled out his K-Bar, then very slowly, he moved to the edge of the stand of tropical grass and carefully cut a few loose leaves that came off the main stalks and were blocking the view forward. The leaves fell silently to the ground, and he carefully peered around big stalks.

The kick caught him right across the face. His helmet shield was designed as a both a screen on which his tactical information could be displayed as well as to protect him from fire and offer some degree of protection from shrapnel. It was not designed to absorb the full impact of a kick.

The faceshield was driven back into his face, smashing his nose, but the force of the kick was spread out over a larger area than had the PLA soldier's kick directly contacted him across his face. Pete was knocked to the ground, and his M4 went flying back into the bushes.

Surprised, his nose aflame, but not really stunned, he grabbed the K-Bar, which had fallen beside him, and jumped up. The PLA soldier was in mid-jump doing some sort of flying back kick.

Pete had received not only the normal Marine MCMAP hand-to-hand combat training but also advanced training as a member of Recon. However, in the split second when he saw that booted foot coming his way, none of that training came into play, and instinct simply took over. He ducked while raising his hand, the one with the knife in it.

Instead of impacting on Pete's head, the soldier's leg impacted on the knife at the lower calf, just above his boot. While the kick was jarring, most of the force of the kick drove the knife deeper into the soldier's flesh where it essentially rode up his fibula, slicing his calf as clean as if a butcher might have done. The K-Bar rode up to the soldier's knee where his momentum knocked the knife out of Pete's hand.

The soldier fell to the ground, grasping at his leg which was spouting a bright crimson fountain. It was then that Pete saw the rifle slung across the soldier's back. Why the soldier had decided to go Kung Fu on him or why he was out on the path alone were questions that flashed through Pete's mind as he reached down to draw his Colt. His right hand was numb from the kick, so he had to transfer the .45 to his left hand. But at this range, which hand he used didn't matter. The soldier was in bad shape and had only a moment to try and reach around to his rifle when Pete fired two rounds into his chest. Without body armor, the rounds made a messy work of him.

With the two rounds breaking the silence, shouts sounded in front of him, foreign shouts. A burst of rounds came flying from down the path. Pete would swear later that the rounds sounded like bees going past his ear as he dove back behind the stand of grass, scrambling to get his rifle. His right hand was still numb, but he needed that M4.

He could hear the several sets of footsteps running as his left hand closed on his rifle and he struggled to swing around and face his enemies. He knew he wasn't going to make it, but he had to try.

Another burst of fire in back of him opened up, and he turned to see one PLA soldier fall on the path, the upper part of his body flopping past the stand of grass to lie just two feet from him. Pete looked back to see Gunny Sloan and LCpl Viejes charging down the path, rifles a blazing.

"Come on, sir!" his gunny shouted, pulling him up.

Pete didn't need any encouragement. Together, the three Marines sprinted back down the path.

When they saw Cpl Schmidt at the side of the path, weapon at the ready, they dived off the path and into the jungle.

"Are you an idiot, Lieutenant? That was a pretty fucking stupid thing to do!" Gunny Sloan shouted, his anger evident.

1stLt Peter Van Slyke didn't have a comeback to his platoon sergeant. The Gunny was absolutely right.

Chapter 1

Pagasa Island, The Spratly Islands
Two days earlier

"OK, *padir*. I got to go. Give *madir* my love."

Analiza's father kissed his hand, then held it up to the cam on his side as she clicked off the connection. While she was glad that SMART provided a free connection for residents of Pagasa, it was not the same thing as being home. She missed her family. She looked forward to December when she could go home for three whole weeks, three weeks of family and friends, of seeing strangers, for goodness sakes. With only 300 residents in Kalayaan town, everyone knew everyone else. Everybody and everything was the same. Sometimes Analiza prayed that something, anything, would happen to break the monotony.

Staring at the now dark computer monitor, she wondered yet once again if the separation from family and friends was worth it. It wasn't the job itself, which she actually enjoyed. The pay was certainly good, more than she could ever earn anywhere else in the Philippines as a teacher. Most of all, even as a civilian, Analiza was proud to be serving her country. But like all residents, she knew she was on the island merely to stake the country's claim to it, and more importantly, to the huge gas reserves and rich fishing grounds surrounding this region of the Spratlys.

She got up, nodded to Bong, the young café clerk, then stepped out into the night. As usual, the pollution-free air was clear, and the stars were bright. Yes, a few things were better here than in Manila, or even her hometown of Cebu. She could never see so many stars at night back in Manila. And traffic? A traffic jam here was when two people bumped into each other while walking into the grocery store.

Even though it was quite late, Analiza wasn't concerned about walking to her small apartment. That was another thing that was better here. It was safe. This wasn't just because of the garrison of 40 soldiers on the island. Since every civilian was screened and the population was limited, crime was almost unheard of.

A breeze kicked up, blowing her long brown hair across her face. Pushing it back, she glanced across the runway at the small dock on the east side. It was rare when they had a boat there, especially a foreign boat. Almost everything on the island arrived by air, and except for a few small privately owned bangkas, the small boats belonging to residents and used to go to the reef to fish, larger boats rarely pulled into port on the island.

Gossip was one of the island residents' Olympic sports, so there was no such thing as a secret. The boat at the dock was a fishing boat from Taiwan that had developed serious engine problems and needed to make an emergency docking in order to effect repairs. Why the boat was in Filipino waters was not explained, but the Republic of China and the Philippines, along with Vietnam and Malaysia, had an uneasy alliance with regards to the Spratlys. With The People's Republic of China claiming the entire group, it made sense for the smaller players to support one another. So even though the mayor had been suspicious regarding in which waters the boat had been fishing, it was granted docking rights.

The runway itself was dark, but a lone light illuminated the guard watching over the boat. It was too far away to see who it was, though. Analiza wondered if it might be Alan; whoever it was, he had the right build to be him.

Analiza had just turned twenty-four, still young, by Filipina standards, but in a country in which the family held such primacy, she was anxious to start her own family. Her mother, after all, had married at sixteen. But with a father who worked as a merchant marine, her family had the cash to send both her and her brother to school, and so boys and dating were out of the question while she was still studying. Now, however, she was out of school with a well-paying job. And Alan, well, he might not be the one, but Analiza thought it might be fun finding out if he was. The pickings might be slim on the island, but with 40 soldiers, most young and fit, these just might be the best odds she would ever face.

She laughed at the thought, and that emboldened her. Why not just saunter over there, a girl just taking a walk, right? "Good" girls, she knew might not be so open, but what could it hurt?

She made her way across the runway to the water's edge, then turned left and continued on as if taking a stroll. She kept looking ahead to see who had guard duty. With fifteen soldiers off the island tonight on their weekly check/resupply/changing-of-the-guard of Likas, she knew the chances were at least decent that the guard was Alan. Only the junior soldiers would be assigned to the duty, and Alan wouldn't be going to Likas until the following week.

When she got to about a hundred yards out, the soldier turned his head, and a little thrill ran through her. It was Alan. He stood the bright light and couldn't see her yet, so she brushed her hair back with her hands and looked down at her clothes. She hadn't dressed to kill when she left for the internet café: brown shorts, a loose, ratty t-shirt that didn't quite meet the top of her shorts, and flip-flops. The gap between the shorts and shirt was her style. She was quite slender and tended to dress to keep attention on her waist rather than her less-than-generous breasts. But she wished she were wearing something nicer.

"Hi Alan, is that you?" she asked innocently as she came up.

Alan jumped, then wheeled around, only relaxing as Analiza walked into the circle of light.

"What are you doing here?" he asked, a smile creasing his face.

"Oh, I couldn't sleep, so I decided to take a walk. I didn't realize you had guard duty," she said, trying to keep her voice innocent.

"Someone has to...."

Analiza stared, not quite understanding as shadows seemed to jump out at Alan, cutting the words off in his throat. The shadows materialized into three men, one in back of Alan with his arm around the Filipino soldier's neck and the other two rushing in front of him.

The three men moved with dangerous, violent grace, but Alan wasn't a pushover. The soldiers stationed in the Spratlys were among the country's best, and one reason Alan had caught Analiza's eye was that he was so, well, so much a man. Alan reached back to gouge his attacker's eyes and somehow grabbed enough of the man's ears to bring his attacker up and over his back as he jerked himself forward. The assailant landed hard on his back on the ground, and Alan lunged forward, striking at the man's exposed neck.

The blow never got there. There was a soft chuff, almost insignificant, as one man pointed a handgun at Alan and fired. Alan fell on top of the prone man, limp and lifeless.

Analiza was having a difficult time understanding what was going on. Why were Taiwanese fishermen attacking Alan? Then their uniforms registered. They were soldiers, too. Pagasa was being attacked!

While The Republic of China technically claimed all of the Spratlys, the two countries had an understanding, what with the People's Republic of China being their strategic adversary over the island group. So why attack?

The two upright soldiers pushed Alan's body off the third man, pulling him upright, voices jabbering in what she recognized as Chinese. With the way his body flopped, she knew for certain that Alan was dead. She gasped and stepped back.

Three sets of eyes swiveled to her. It was as if they had forgotten she was standing there. It was only then that something else registered. Instead of Taiwan's red flag with the blue and yellow star thingy in the middle, over the boat now flew the red flag with yellow star of the People's Republic. This wasn't a Taiwan attack. This was China invading them!

The garrison had to be warned. She wheeled around and started to run. For a moment she thought they might let her go, just a helpless girl in the darkness. In seconds, however, she heard the heavy footfalls of someone chasing her.

Her left flip-flop tore and fell off, the hard coral runway digging into her foot with each step, but she couldn't stop. She had to warn them. She could see the lights ahead, but they were a long way off, and the footsteps were right behind her. She opened her mouth to scream, knowing no one could hear her yet, when the heavy body crashed into her from behind, driving her face onto the runway and sending her into blackness.

Chapter 2
Pattaya, Thailand

1st Lt Peter Van Slyke walked into the Fantasy Sports Bar on Walking Street, peering around to find his group. It was quite late, but the street was well-lit with garish neon signs, so with the low light levels inside, it took a few moments for his eyes to adjust.

"Welcome, sir!" a petite waitress almost sang in a high, lilting voice as she came over to greet him.

This was a sports bar, complete with three pool tables and a number of televisions currently showing various sports, ranging from what looked, at first glance, to be soccer, billiards, and badminton. He shifted his attention to the waitress. She was cute, no doubt about that. She might have come head-high to his chest, and she might weigh 90 pounds soaking wet, but in her cheerleader-looking outfit, well, Pete hoped she was a good omen on what might happen later on in the night. He had heard enough about the surplus of women in Pattaya on the ship before pulling in, and though he was normally somewhat shy around the fairer sex, he figured that here, his wallet might trump his appearance, and he was looking forward to that. But first, he had to attend to a tradition.

He was just about to tell her he was meeting a group when a voice called out, "Glad you decided to join us, there, lieutenant of Marines. Why don't you get your scarred ass over here and buy us a round."

He looked to the right to see Capt Niimoto, along with the rest of his old security guard detachment, sitting at a table, bottles of Chang already in evidence. Pete was normally quite conscious of the huge scar that distorted the entire left side of his face, but the captain had an equally impressive one on his neck and face, courtesy of his Somalia adventure. So from him, he didn't mind the barb.

9

"Sorry sir," he said as he pulled out a chair. "The colonel wanted me to finish my gear inspection before libo, and I only now got it done."

"You know what they say there, lieutenant. 'Excuses are like assholes. Everybody has one, and they all stink.' I thought I trained you better than that," SgtMaj Jacob McCardle told him, Chang in hand.

"Well, now that Ricky Recon has chosen to grace us with his presence, as soon as he gets his drink, we can get to the matter at hand," the captain said, motioning over for a waitress.

Pete looked at the gathered Marines, all of them from his old security guard detachment in New Delhi. There was Captain Anthony Niimoto, then a sergeant, but now the senior Marine in this elite group. Next to him was SgtMaj McCardle, who had been a gunny and the detachment commander at the time. Gunny Mac had been a good guy, but not the most aggressive Marine around. SgtMaj Mac had seemingly grown into his rank, and he seemed more assured than Pete remembered him.

Stepchild was there, too. Sgt Harrington Steptoe, the tall, soft-looking Marine who was now the captain's company comm chief. Next to him sat GySgt Ian Harwood. Ian had gotten out with the embassy staff and guests and hadn't taken part in the fight, but he had still been part of the detachment. Only Mahmoud Saad was missing, doing whatever he was doing back as Ft. Meade. A lance corporal at the time, he was already a staff sergeant and doing some sort of secret squirrel stuff at NSA.

These were the men with whom Pete had formed an unbreakable bond. They were all well-known throughout the Corps, of course, being largely responsible for not only keeping the president alive but in bringing back the Corps as a viable combat unit. But their bond was on a more personal level, that of men who had fought together and lost friends. Each year, on the anniversary of the takeover of the embassy, those who could got together to toast their fallen comrades. A few times it had been over the internet, and several times, the commandant had joined them, given honorary status as the man who had led the rescue mission. But this, their eighth ceremony, was the first time that they were meeting overseas.

And this was the first time that they would be saluting Joseph Child. SSgt Child had passed away a few months earlier at his Detroit VA hospice.

Pete's Chang arrived, and now that they were all charged, SgtMaj Mac took over.

"To Joseph Child!" he declared, raising up his bottle of Chang.

"To Joseph Child!" the rest of the New Delhi vets chorused, raising their own bottles of beer.

Pete looked over at Stepchild. He had been devoted to Child, hence his "Stepchild" nickname. The big Marine tilted up his bottle, but a tear could be seen rolling down his cheek.

One by one, SgtMaj Mac went down the list. Seth Croker. Tracy " Little Mac" McAllister. Jesus Rodriguez. Samantha Ashely. Ivy "Princess" Ramon. Mike Fallgatter. Greg Chen. Shareetha Wynn. Each one got an individual toast.

Then they went to the others. MAJ Defilice, the assistant Army attaché. Drayton Bajinski, the USAID officer. Capt Leon-Guerro, their company XO who had been there at the time. And Mr. Dravid, the old Indian man who was treated as little more than a servant, but whose sacrifice might have kept the president alive long enough for the rescue.

Pete couldn't help but feel a lump in his throat. And, as usual, he felt a bit of guilt that he had survived when so many others hadn't. If he hadn't been shot in the face at the very beginning of the siege, he probably wouldn't have survived. But as he was badly injured, the others had to take the more dangerous missions, and most of them didn't make it.

With the roll call finished, each of them sat back, quiet. No one had to speak. Their presence alone gave each other support.

For the thousandth time, Peter Van Slyke wondered about his position in life, in the Corps. He was the sixth generation of Van Slykes to serve as a Marine. His grand-father had earned a Medal of Honor in Vietnam. His father had been killed in Iraq. There had been little doubt that Pete would become a Marine, even when the

Marines had been cut back to little more than a ceremonial guard. And then, as a PFC, he was thrust into the embassy takeover. As a result, he had been given a presidential appointment to the Naval Academy, despite his horribly disfigured face that had still required several surgeries and therapy while he was a midshipman.

His notoriety at the Academy helped him, and despite the fact that his grades, while good, were not at the top of the class, he was appointed as the second set brigade commander. Taking his commission, he excelled at The Basic School, then at the Infantry Officers Course. All of this forced him to put up a front, to act like he was confident when he was actually self-conscious about his face almost to the point of not being able to function. He knew that eyes were on him, staring at him. And that made him want to freeze up, to put a hood over his head *a la* the elephant man.

Being assigned to B 1/7 as a platoon commander, though, had given him at least a degree of confidence. His Marines seemed to like him, even to be proud of the fact that their commander had seen combat. And he loved Thursdays, when, if they were not in the field, their PT was sports. It was like he had his own private football team.

He had made an uneventful pump, doing exercises with the Japanese, Koreans, and Filipinos, but he had never pulled into one of the "good" liberty ports like Pattaya. After getting back to Pendleton, he went to one of the semi-annual tryouts for recon, and not surprisingly, he was selected, not having too much difficulty with the RIP and BRC or dive school after that. This was now his first deployment as a recon platoon commander, assigned to the 15th MEU.

The other four Marines were all with the BLT, with Mac as the battalion sergeant major, Capt Niimoto and Stepchild with Kilo Company, and Ian Harwood as the supply chief. Pete's presence with the MEU was a coincidence, but he knew that SgtMaj Mac or Capt Niimoto had pulled strings to get the rest of them assigned together. The captain even had his old platoon sergeant, Burke Davidson, the guy who was awarded the Medal of Honor in Somalia for saving his ass, assigned back to him as his company first sergeant.

Slowly, they started talking again, enjoying the camaraderie. New Delhi was not mentioned, but life in general was. Capt Niimoto brought out his tablet to show photos of Amalyn, his new daughter. She was his fourth kid. When Pete was with him in New Delhi, the then Sgt Niimoto was a goof ball, a laughing surfer dude from San Diego. It was odd seeing him now as such a proud family man.

The captain had been good for Pete, though. Shortly after getting underway, the two had had a long discussion, catching up on old times. When Pete asked him about surgeries, the captain told him he had none after he was stabilized. He didn't want surgery for purely cosmetic reasons. He called his own disfigurements his "Heidelberg scars." Pete even thought that the captain might be more proud of this scars than his Navy Cross or Silver Star, if that made sense. At that moment, Pete vowed that he'd have no more surgery on his own face. It was what it was.

Gunny Harwood was getting a few sheets to the wind. If he got too far gone, Pete knew SgtMaj Mac would get him back to the ship. The MEU commanding officer's prime directive for the three days of liberty was that there were to be no, repeat no liberty incidents. As no one wanted any liberty curtailed, it was "watch out for each other time."

The waitress brought Pete another bottle of Chang. It was only his second, but as he watched her walk away with a nice wiggle in her butt, he reminded himself of what he wanted to do later, and he didn't want to be drunk while doing it.

He was wondering how he would make his escape and go to one of the more adult-oriented bars when 1stSgt Davidson walked up. Pete had not talked to him yet, but he recognized the only active duty Marine with the Medal of Honor.

"Skipper," he said, leaning in to Capt Niimoto. "You need to get back. The SP's are going to be rounding up everyone for a recall, but you need to get back and meet with the CO ASAP."

Capt Niimoto looked up with a confused look on his face. "Why, what's up?"

The 1stSgt looked around the bar, then leaned closer and said so only those at the table could hear, "It looks like the Chinese may have invaded the Spratlys."

Chapter 3
Beijing, China

General Li Zhiyuan, Deputy Chief of Staff of the People's Liberation Army, left the tall General Staff Headquarters, his driver wending his way through the bustling traffic. The architect had designed the headquarters to look like it was seemingly balanced on a point, like a reverse pyramid. To General Li, it had always seemed to him that it symbolized the PLA, precariously balancing itself and the needs of the nation against the political types from the Central Military Commission, the party and state officials who controlled China's vast and powerful armed forces. General Li was a party member, of course. He could not have attained his present rank had he not been. But he always thought the military and the defense of the country should be left to those in the military, not the politicians, especially the politicians who openly embraced western culture and economic growth.

And now, he was the one doing the balancing. He knew the way forward for China, and with a few like-minded individuals and the support of loyal subordinates, and with the push from the still unknown person or persons higher in the power structure of the country, he had taken action, action that would vault China into its proper position as the world's premier super power.

He had been pleased though, that in the early morning briefing for General Chen Jun, the PLA chief of staff, no word had yet leaked out of the operation. He knew it would get out soon, but he wanted the operation presented as a *fait accompli*, not something still in process.

His fingers drummed on his knee as they slowly made their way through the morning commuter traffic to the nondescript white building that was the actual nerve center for the operation. He hated wasting time even when things were routine; with the operation in full swing, it was even worse. If there had been any way to control the operation from the headquarters, he would have done it. But there was no way that could be kept secret, and he could not afford the CMC getting wind of it and closing the operation down before it could succeed.

The driver finally pulled in front of their destination. No one rushed forward to open his door—General Li did not need nor allow for such symbols of subservience. He stepped out of the car and walked into the building. The lone soldier at the simple desk came to attention and saluted before taking a key and opening the door behind him, a door that looked like tens of thousands of other doors into the city, leading into shops, homes, and offices.

General Li had thought to get some counter-terrorism experts to maintain security, but the Intermediate Action Unit personnel were all technically part of the police force, not the Army, and thinking that hiding in plain sight was a better option, he had elected to go with a single PLA soldier manning the entrance.

While the hallway of the building looked like every other building, the room into which he strode would have made the National Space Administration proud. It was bright, almost blindingly white, and spotless. Various computer hubs buzzed with activity with about 30 people engrossed at their stations. It was hard to believe that this was the heart of the action that was thrusting China forward into the future.

The target of his attention was looking over the shoulder of another technician, focused on whatever information was being gathered on that man's computer. Sung Wenyan was in his mid-30's and looked like a shopkeeper. At about 180 cm, he probably weighed 80 kg and had a continual smile cemented to his face. That smile might fool others into thinking he was a nice, congenial fellow, but Li knew that it hid a pretty cold and calculating mind. "Wenyan" might mean refined and virtuous, but the man himself was anything but that.

He was brilliant, though, to give credit where credit was due. His problem was in not using his brilliance for the good of the people but rather for his own gain. A master programmer, Wenyan had bedeviled companies and government agencies for several years by hacking into their systems. Initially, he never caused much damage nor received material gain from his escapades, but he left calling cards to announce his success. As time went on and he became bolder, however, he did manage to siphon several million yuan into an off-shore bank account from the Department of Interior's accounting department. His downfall came when he hacked into the PLA's most secure system, playing a pornographic video of him and a woman on a loop that took the PLA's best computer minds almost three hours to stop. Both he and the woman had worn hoods, but like many criminals, Wenyan couldn't keep a secret, and when he bragged to a friend, that friend had turned him in.

Sung Wenyan had been quickly tried and sentenced to a bullet in the back of the head—only, he hadn't been killed. He had been stashed in Qincheng Prison, where mostly political prisoners were kept.

An anonymous phone call had led General Li to Sung. It was the nature of Chinese politics that such calls were best not ignored, so he had taken a trip to the prison to meet the hacker. It was immediately clear to him that Sung was an asset that was too valuable to waste. He made an offer that Sung could not refuse, and by pulling his own strings, got him transferred into Army custody.

Sung was still a prisoner, albeit a prisoner with authority, one whom General Li kept plied with good-looking and accommodating women (all loyal PLA soldiers, of course) and Jack Daniels, Sung's beverage of choice. Li didn't trust Sung, pure and simple. He didn't mind the womanizing and drinking. While General Li chose not to poison his own body with alcohol, in his opinion, one of a man's duties in life was to give pleasure to women, to take a woman, any woman, and reduce her to a grateful, if quivering, exhausted state. General Li's secret hubris was his ability to do this, something that he had undertaken to achieve with as much single-mindedness as he undertook most tasks. So he understood this need, even if the reports he was given by the soldiers assigned to this task were that

Wenyan was perhaps more interested in his own gratification than that of the women's.

That Wenyan had this weakness was perhaps not surprising. As one of the 40 million or so "bare branches," men who had little hope of finding a wife due to the long years of illegal abortions of female fetuses, he was just one man who contributed to the growing social ills of the country. He may not have the courage to have joined one of the *New Nien* gangs, those groups of desperate young men who controlled prostitution, smuggling of sex slaves from neighboring countries, drugs, kidnapping, rape, and all sorts of other crimes. But he took out his frustration in his own way, trying to obtain wealth and women, and with his weaknesses, the general could control him.

General Li had a disdain for the bare branches and what they were doing to the nation. Just as the original *Nien* gangs had contributed to the fall of the Qing Dynasty, so the *New Nien* were tearing down China. It was not lost on him, though, that what he was doing could be a relief valve, not only providing China with much needed resources, but starting the country down a path that could lead to new territory, territory that needed young Chinese men to administer.

Despite his disdain for the *New Nien* and other bare branches, he was more than willing to use any of them to further the nation's causes. It wasn't that he trusted any of them. What specifically rendered Wenyan as someone who could not be trusted was that he used his gifts for his own ends, either for money or fame. He did not use them to better the Chinese people. For that, General Li could not forgive him nor trust him. Use him, however, that he could do.

And General Li Zhiyuan, Deputy Chief of Staff of the PLA, was perhaps in a better position to use Wenyan than most anyone else. Because of his position, Li was one of the few people in the country to know one closely held state secret: China had back doors into most of the world's satellites, communications systems, and even military software.

Over the years China had been taking over more and more manufacturing from other countries, and this included in electronics. Part of this was because of price and quality, part of it was because China had long ago taken over the production of rare earths from the USA, those critical elements needed for most high tech applications.

Chinese wizards had developed components that would pass the most rigorous inspections. They would function as designed by the customers, but when subjected to a very tight and specific frequency, the housings of the components would act as simple on-off switches, allowing Chinese programming to enter and hijack various functions.

This was a huge leap from August 30, 2007 when the Chinese had caused a B-52 at Minot Air Force Base to be loaded with six nuclear cruise missiles and take off. It took three hours for the Americans to realize what had happened and divert the plane to land at Barksdale AFB in Louisiana. This in itself was a significant step forward from earlier in the year when Chinese hackers caused Vice President Cheney's 757 to land at Singapore.

It took both hackers and American corporations sub-contracting out vital components to Chinese companies for them to be able to do this. After these two incidents, some politicians in the US, Japan, the EU, and other countries objected to vital parts in communications, military equipment, and defense-related satellites being "Wal-Marted," as the term became known, but the bottom line ruled the roost, especially as any part could be supposedly tested. And if Chinese-made components were not ordered, then they could be slipped in and substituted through bribery, or in one case, by a brilliant act of subterfuge, something right out of a Hollywood movie.

With this ability to open up windows into satellites and communications hubs, someone like Sung Wenyan could essentially take control over them. And this was the final piece of the puzzle. For years, General Li had chaffed at the handcuffs placed on his country when dealing with the rest of the world. They bowed and scraped to the African savages in order to get their raw materials. They paid exorbitant prices to Australia, the US, and Russia for more raw materials. They had the power to take what they wanted, but the politicians would rather play diplomatic games.

Someone, though, someone probably as high as a member of the Central Committee, had given him the information about Sung Wenyan. Someone had sent him a link to a study that had advocated China's taking control of the Wanli Shitang, what the rest of the world called The Spratlys. That someone or someones had to be like-minded with him. Whoever it was wanted him to take action.

He had taken the hint. For him, the new China would start with the Wanli Shitang. Chinese had been in these islands for over 2,500 years, and it wasn't right that a collection of small, weak countries could keep China from the much needed gas and oil reserves, much less the rich fishing grounds that could help feed China's billion-and-a-half people.

Last night, it had started. Thitu Island had fallen quickly, the special forces unit from The Sword of Southern China getting on the island on a Taiwan-flagged fishing boat. There were no friendly casualties and only a handful of Filipino soldiers killed before the rest, as well as the civilians, were captured.

Things had not gone so well on Taiping, where the Taiwan Marines had not been taken by surprise. Even though the electronic measures had functioned as planned, Marines with rifles, 120mm mortars, and 40mm autocannons did not need advanced electronics. The larger Sword of Southern China special forces team assigned to take the island had been wiped out before they could even land.

Taiping was still cut off from all means of communications, but now, General Li had to give the order to divert the *Changbai Shan* and the *Jinggan Shan*, two of the PLA Navy's Type 071 Amphibious Transport Docks, along with their embarked 1,800 Marines, to the stubborn island.

The longer this took, the more likely it was that word would get out. General Li needed the Wanli Shitang completely in Chinese hands before the world realized what had happened. The Central Committee couldn't back down then.

"So, Mr. Sung, what's your report?" he simply asked the hacker.

Sung Wenyan turned around, then nodded his head respectfully, something the general knew was an act.

"General Li, by all accounts, we are still cloaked in secrecy. The enemy satellites are all showing what we want them to show, and there has been no alarm from anywhere."

"Sir, what about the outgoing burst from Taiping?" asked the computer operator at whose station they stood.

"What was that?" demanded the general.

"Ah, nothing to be concerned about, sir," put in Sung hurriedly. "There might have been a short burst of static from Taiping before we gained control of the communications nexus. But there has been no response from the Taiwan renegades, so there is no reason to be concerned."

General Li looked into Sung Wenyan's eyes. There was something more going on there, he thought. But what was done was done.

"What about Thitu Island? What are the reports?"

"Sir, the glorious soldiers of the Sword of Southern China bask in their accomplishments in taking back our land from the Filipinos. However, the water and electricity have been sabotaged, and well, the exalted soldiers need engineers to fix those. Communications are well and truly down there, so we have to rely on the special forces team's internal communications."

With all the "gloriouses" and "exalteds," Sung was spouting perfect revolutionary rhetoric, but Li was not fooled. The man had a pretty high opinion of himself, and the remark about the soldiers not being able to fix the water production was a jab at what he thought of their mental capabilities.

He wished for the hundredth time that this command center was back at headquarters, or that he could at least use his cell phone to get updates. He had to get back for another inane meeting on procurement when all he wanted to do was to sit there, leading the operation. He had good men out at sea and in the attack, but here, at the heartbeat, he had a criminal in charge. That didn't sit well with him. Perhaps he should have brought in someone else, like Col Lian, for one, to camp out in the control center until they could bring everything out into the open.

"Mr. Sung, I have to be back at headquarters. I will return in two hours. If anything happens that needs my attention, have someone go across the street and give me a missed call, and I will get back here immediately," he instructed the hacker.

Just a little bit longer, he thought to himself as he left the building. *Then I can stop this sneaking around and let the world know what we've done.*

Chapter 4
Aboard the USS Makin Island

1stLt Peter Van Slyke edged forward a bit to get a better view. It was packed pretty tight. All the senior Marines and the available Navy officers and chiefs were crowded into the briefing room while LCDR Grace Sullivan, the Task Force intelligence officer went on with her brief.

"So, as you can see from this timeline, at 2315 local time, an ROC Army comm tech received what started as an emergency message over his system. It cut off immediately as if a switch was turned off. He tried to re-establish the link, but nothing was going through. A few moments later, a call on another circuit gave a routine message that normal communications would be interrupted for a short period while some repairs were being made.

"Normally, that might make sense, but the tech was worried that there was some sort of emergency unknown to the garrison at large, so he tried to contact two ROC ships in the area, but all comm was down, not just to the Marine garrison.

"At 2322, this was reported up the chain of command, and a routine scan of satellite photos was ordered."

She flashed up on the screen a photo of the lights of an island surrounded by darkness.

"This was taken by an ROC satellite at 2320."

She then put up another photo so that both were side-by-side.

"The one on the right was taken at 2305. Note the cloud cover, cover that is not present on the one on the left. This raised some immediate flags, so the ROC armed forces command contacted the Pentagon to ask for their help in figuring out what was wrong. As it turned out, it wasn't only the ROC satellites that were affected. Each US and, as we found out later, UK and Japanese satellites were also affected in the same way. Running our data through analysis, we quickly determined that what we were seeing, real time, was an exact duplicate of what had happened one month before. Our satellites were being spoofed."

She paused for effect, noting the concerned looks around the room as the significance of that sunk in.

"There was also an anomaly concerning two PLA Navy ships in the region, the *Changbai Shan* and the *Jinggan Shan*, which are Type 071 Amphibious Transport Docks. "

She pulled up another satellite photo.

"We track all major combatants, as you know. Well, the computers back at DIA pulled up a small glitch, an anomaly on their track.

"We also contacted the Philippines Armed Forces to ask about their forces in the region, and they informed us that they were in the middle of a communications interruption. So that makes comm problems for both the ROC and the Philippines?" she said, her rising voice making it more of a question than a statement.

"Given all of this put together, the Pentagon issued orders for us to get underway, for the *Gerald R. Ford* Battle Group to steam south from the Sea of Japan, and for the 13th Air Force at Anderson AFB on Guam to go on alert. As the commander told you earlier, at the time, it was better to be prepared even if we didn't know what was going on.

"But now, this is new information. At 0730 local time, the *USS Mississippi*, one of our attack subs, was able to come in close to Thitu Island and take photos through its periscope. Initially, the island seemed deserted. However, the *Mississippi* eventually took this photo."

The photo came on the screen. It was clearly taken from long distance, but just as clearly, a soldier in uniform could be seen smoking a cigarette outside a building.

"This is a soldier in the PLA, in fact, a special forces soldier from what is known as 'The Sword of Southern China.' And this confirms that whatever is happening, the People's Republic of China is behind it.

"I should point out, though, that while the *Mississippi* took the photo at 0730, they could not get it to us until almost four hours later. Whatever is affecting communications over the Spratlys, it can even keep a nuke sub from communicating while it is in its range. It can get out simple text messages using its Extremely Low Frequency antenna, but as most of you know, a sub cannot send images nor receive via the ELF, and we needed NSA to confirm the photo before we could now act on it. "

There were more murmurs as this sunk in. If the Chinese were in back of this, and if they could take over satellites and knock out communications, what else could they do?

"I will be updating everything we know on a continuous basis. And now, I'm going to turn it over to Commander Belling, the Ops Officer."

Pete leaned back to take it all in. Before the float he wondered if they might have a contingency somewhere. He never imagined that he could be staring at the brink of WWIII.

Chapter 5
Over the South China Sea

Major Camino "Ting" Opena looked over to his wingman, Lieutenant Senior Grade Joseph Acacio, as they hurtled over the water towards Pagasa Island in their Saab Gripens. Both pilots were assigned to the 570th Tactical Composite Wing at Puerto Princesa, the unit responsible for not only Palawan, but also for defense of Philippines' assets in the Spratlys.

Ting really didn't know what to expect on this reconnaissance mission. He had been briefed, of course. With communications down over Pagasa and Likas, it made sense that a recon overflight be made, but if the Americans were right, there might be a Chinese threat right now on the islands. Ting's mission was to get eyeballs on the target to see if there was anything different from what the Filipino weather satellite was currently showing.

He checked the gauges on his old Gripen. The Gripen was a reliable plane, but this one had been purchased back in 2014, and it was feeling its age. For the thousandth time, he wished the Air Force had bought the American F-16 back then, but the bean counters back in Manila objected to the upkeep costs of the Fighting Falcon, and the Swedes promised a much cheaper supply chain for the Gripens. So the serviceable Gripen became the Air Force fighter, replacing the even more ancient F5. If there were Chinese on the island, though, Ting didn't look forward to any sort of confrontation with any of the top-of-the-line Chinese fighters.

The flight from Puerto Princesa to Pagasa was only 240 miles, a little over 30 minutes in his Gripen, so he knew he should be coming up on the island soon. The plan was for both aircraft to make a pass from south to north, then bear west before looping around and passing over the runway from west to east.

Although not in his orders, he and Joseph had decided to keep off the radio unless it was absolutely necessary. If there were Chinese there, it would do no good to let them know they were coming.

Ting looked out of his canopy and signaled to Joseph that they needed to begin their descent. Joseph gave him a thumbs up, and so Ting started bringing his Gripen down, knowing Joseph would stay on his wing.

It was low tide, so he could see Half Moon Shoal below him as he passed over. It wouldn't be long now.

He brought his Gripen down to 5,000 feet, low enough to get a good view of the island as he flew over. Bringing his plane to a heading of 3-3-2, he only had to keep in a straight line to fly right over it.

Suddenly, his entire cockpit control went dark. Panic swept through him. This had never happened to him before. He cursed the choice of the politicians who had decided the Gripen was "good enough," and he went through his restart procedures while his plane began an ungainly glide down towards the sea. Nothing seemed to work. He tried again, but his cockpit panel remained ominously dark. Looking out, he could see that he was perhaps 1,000 feet up, although it was harder to tell than if he had been over land.

He knew he had to punch out. He spared a glance up to find Joseph, knowing the mission was now up to him, but he couldn't spot his wingman. There was no time. He reached down and pulled on the ejection seat release. This was essentially an explosive charge, not connected to the plane's power. The explosion slammed Ting into the seat, or rather slammed the seat up into his butt. It felt like he had been hit with a club, and he was thrown into the air at something like 500 miles per hour, he figured, based on the plane slowing down a bit with the engines shut off.

He was stunned, and his right arm was numb, but when he felt the opening shock of his chute opening, he let out a breath he hadn't even realized he was holding. He was going to get wet, but at least he should make it.

He looked back up to try and catch sight of Joseph's plane, hoping he went on with the mission and was not coming back to see what happened. He could report back to base, and they would send a Huey out to get him.

He was surprised, then, to see the bright orange and white parachute of another ejection seat about a mile away, making its own descent into the water. That parachute came from a Gripen, he knew, so Joseph had also suffered the same catastrophic cockpit failure.

Their Gripens might be old, but they were reliable, and two of them didn't fail like that at the same time. A sense of foreboding rushed through him as he drifted down closer to the water. If this was a deliberate attack of some sort, then what was going on?

Chapter 6
Beijing

General Chen Jun, the Chief of Staff for the People's Liberation Army, strode back to his office. To say he was angry would be an understatement. The general was a powerful man in China, and he was not used to being called before the Central Military Commission like a student called before the school principle. Especially when the accusations were groundless.

China invading the Wanli Shitang? It was preposterous. This was clearly a political move by the Americans, the Taiwan government, and the Filipinos. To what end, he wasn't sure, but they had manufactured some inconclusive "evidence" that the American ambassador had presented to the general secretary. What made matters worse was that the general secretary, in his additional position of chairman of the CMC, seemed to give the accusations some credence.

His aide rushed in front of him, opening doors and getting people out of his way. The aide was used to the general's famed temper, and he was trying to keep a lid on any potential explosions.

General Chen burst through the double doors to his outer office.

"Where's General Li," he asked, handing his cap to a waiting aide.

"Sir, he left the headquarters on a family emergency, and he isn't answering his phone," Captain Lin Shi Wei, told him, her eyes downcast, waiting for the outburst.

"And so you stopped at that? I told you I wanted him now. Send a driver to his house, and I don't care if his wife or his daughter is on her deathbed, I want him here now." He looked around the office. "Senior Colonel Wang, I'm going to want the entire general officer staff in my conference room in fifteen minutes. I trust that you can get that done?"

"Yes sir," his junior military aide shouted before rushing to his side office to make the calls.

General Chen went into his inner office and sat down. He would get to the bottom of this and then personally shove the accusations up the American ambassador's ass.

Chapter 7
Over the South China Sea

Lieutenant Colonel Marco Salcedo looked about the big C-130 as it made its way to Pagasa Island. He had almost 160 soldiers crammed into the big bird, far more than its official capacity of 92 combat-ready troops, but by packing the soldiers in like sardines, they managed to shove them in for the 45-minute flight.

They had been on alert since this morning, and when the two Gripens had disappeared, it looked like things were on hold. But when the OV-10 that had taken off at the same time as the Gripens had stood 20 miles off Pagasa and had taken photos of the island, and when the Hueys had rescued both downed pilots without incident, the powers that be decided that whatever took down the Gripens had to be only aimed at fast movers. So the president himself had ordered the mission.

And with only 15-20 Chinese soldiers on Pagasa, the best they could tell, the 160 soldiers from his battalion would be an overwhelming force, more than enough for the PLA soldiers to just give up without loss of life. Marco got the feeling that perhaps an even more robust option had been considered, but with only one working C-130 available at Puerto Princesa, either waiting for another plane to arrive or perhaps that the response shouldn't be too big as to start an all-out war made this option the best one.

If the PLA soldiers did give up, Marco was under strict orders to ensure none were hurt. The Chinese would have made their statement, and the ball would be then in the politician's court.

Marco had been in combat before, fighting against Abu Sayyaf as a lieutenant and captain. But no one currently serving in the Philippines armed forces had been in full-scale combat. The Navy had had some clashes around Scarborough Shoal and in the

Spratlys, and the Air Force had that one dog fight with the Malaysian Air Force a few years back, but the ground forces hadn't really been called upon to defend the country against a foreign enemy.

Part of him wanted the Chinese to fight back. Even with only a part of his battalion, Marco was sure his men would prevail, and against the Chinese? Well, his future would be assured, either in the Army or in politics. On the other hand, he knew the Philippines could not risk a real war with China, a war that the country could not hope to win.

He knew that actual combat was not likely. But the Philippines was making a statement that it would not be pushed around, and that they would not relinquish their claim to their portion of the islands, the ones in their own territorial waters. And if nothing else, then this operation would be a success.

The big plane banked to the left, ready to make the loop that would bring it aligned with the runway, landing west to east. With the ramp down, his troops would rush out the back and present an overwhelming force to the Chinese who seemed to be centered around Kalayaan town itself. As the C-130 rolled slowly down the airstrip while the troops disembarked, his unit would be essentially on line, able to circle around the town, surrounding it. The line might have some gaps considering the numbers he had with him, but against such a small number of Chinese, it shouldn't matter.

No, the Chinese would have to surrender and without harming any of the civilians or the garrison soldiers they must have surprised and captured.

Marco moved up to the hatch leading up to the cockpit. He wanted an aerial view as they came in. Captain Ibasco was an outstanding officer and would be one of the first out of the plane, and he could be counted upon to get the attack formation going, so Marco felt confident taking the time to get a better view of things as they landed.

As with the OV-10 that did the recon, the C-130's radios quit working as they approached the area. But the plane flew fine.

As he sat down on the small jump seat, the co-pilot leaned over and yelled into his ear, "That's Pagasa Island, sir, right over there."

Marco had been on the island before, but this view was new to him. Ahead, in the distance, the island was clearly visible despite the slight haze. The C-130 was lined up on the runway, slowly making its descent. Off on either wing, two OV-10s flew alongside. The OV-10's were not heavily armed, but their four M60C machine guns and two pods each of 2.75 inch Folding Fin Aerial Rockets still gave him a stronger sense of security.

He looked back into the cargo bay. The ramp was being lowered. The troops were packed in tight, and Marco prayed that the plane didn't hit any turbulence, possibly throwing one of his soldiers out.

He looked back forward, a nervous sense of excitement building. This was where he would make his mark on history, he knew. This was where all of his training, all of his hard work, would come to fruition.

They were only two hundred feet up and possibly half a mile out when there seemed to be an explosion on the island and smoke billowed into the air. But it didn't billow straight up—four fingers of smoke seemed to reach out to them.

It took the pilot's "Oh, shit" to register what was happening. He then knew this wasn't some giant hand reaching out to them, although it might as well have been. He only had time to clutch the silver cross he wore around his neck before his world erupted into heat and flames before going dark.

Chapter 8
Aboard the USS Makin Island

"Pete, you've got to take down the anti-air or we're well and truly fucked," Capt Niimoto told him as he gathered his notes.

"Don't worry, sir, we'll do it," he replied.

Peter Van Slyke was pretty confident about his platoon's capabilities, but he hoped his bravado was not misplaced. Going in without normal comm was worrisome, but the Marines prided themselves on making do.

This mission would be tricky even in optimum conditions. Taking off from the *Makin Island* in an Osprey, they would link up with the *USS Mississippi*, fast rope down to the submarine, then use that platform to insert onto Thitu Island before daylight took away their cover of darkness. The photos they had received from the Philippines Air Force were not the clearest, so it was difficult to make out exactly what kind of anti-aircraft missile battery the Chinese had, but whatever it was, it had to be taken out or Kilo Company would be blown out of the sky like the Filipino C-130 had been.

While his platoon was being inserted, the amphibious group would continue at flank speed towards the Spratlys, and tomorrow, Kilo Company would land and seize control of Thitu while the rest of the MEU would proceed to Taiping to reinforce the ROC Marines who had managed to hold back the first Chinese attempt to take the island.

That was based on the last known intel, of course. The Philippines had been asked to send a an OV-10 over Taiping, and it looked to still be in ROC hands. But somewhere out there, two PLA Navy Amphibious Transport Docks were unaccounted for, and if they arrived and took the beleaguered island first, then all bets were off. A single MEU probably could not take the island back from up to 1,800 PLA troops, so the MEU's orders were to stand off if that happened and let the politicians try to defuse the situation. No one knew if the Chinese would feel the same way with an American MEU on the island, though. Would they back off rather than risk WWIII, or would they forge ahead and try to take it?

India Company was set to take off within 30 minutes to try and get some feet on the ground on Taiping, but the danger zone was after the first Marines hit the ground but before enough forces could be built up to offer a serious opposition to the Chinese. To further complicate things, they still had no comm with the ROC Marines on the island, so there was the threat of friendly fire. The ROC had managed to obtain communications with one patrol boat outside of the blackout area, and it was supposed to precede them and let the garrison know that help was coming, but no one knew what the PLA Navy had in between the island and the boat. So the Philippines Air Force had agreed to send an OV-10 in first and land, letting the ROC Marines know that the Ospreys were friendlies.

The entire communications, satellite, and aircraft issue was causing panic right up to the White House. The MEU S-2 had briefed them that there was a full-court press to get to the bottom of what was happening. All US and allied forces had been put on the highest alert and techs were going over every piece of electronic equipment as well as software to determine just how deep the issue went. Currently, the effect seemed to be limited to around the Spratlys, but if the Chinese could do it there, the feeling was that they could reach anywhere.

The Chinese were denying everything, of course. Their non-involvement had to be considered, but all the evidence, meager as it was, pointed to them. From the anomalies in some of the recorded data to the Filipino overflights, the Chinese were the most likely aggressors. The S2 reported that NOAA had managed to re-power an old weather satellite and was getting it back online, and the initial reports were that it was sending back real-time data, but it would take awhile before it could be re-programmed to acquire militarily useful information.

And if it was not the Chinese, then who? The Spratlys were claimed as a whole or in part by China, Taiwan, the Philippines, Malaysia, Vietnam, and Brunei. Although what had attacked the US systems seemed beyond any current capabilities, the only nation that could possibly have developed those capabilities was the People's Republic of China.

The fact that it was all modern systems that were compromised was not lost on Pete. Older systems had been unaffected. OV-10's and C-130's could fly, even if they could not communicate. The ancient radar installation on Palawan had been able to track aircraft over much of the Spratlys. And now, a 30-year-old weather satellite seemed to be up and running again.

The Marine Corps was no different from any other organization—it relied on high tech for just about everything. Pete felt naked knowing that all the gadgets and weapons that helped make the US military unsurpassed in the world probably would not work on this mission. They most likely no longer had that technological edge. When it got down to it, this might be one US Marine against one PLA soldier, man-to-man, on an even playing field.

He had less than an hour before his platoon was to take off, so he took his leave of Capt Niimoto and left the briefing room. High tech or low, his Marines had to be ready.

Chapter 9

Beijing

General Li took the handset and spoke.

"Senior Captain Chou, I gave the order over 10 hours ago for you to proceed to the objective and take it. Now, I am told that you are still hours away. I put you in command there to ensure there were no foul-ups, yet I see that there are. Can you please explain yourself?"

"General, the *Changbai Shan* has suffered a breakdown of one of its Pielstick engines, and that has seized up one shaft. We are proceeding forward at 12 knots."

General Li did the quick calculation in his head, going from the archaic knots to kilometers before responding, "And the *Jinggan Shan*? Is it also down?"

"No General. It is functioning as normal."

The general tried to control his temper. His authority was stretched further than was legal as it was, and the entire fate of his country was on a precarious perch. He could not afford to alienate the idiot of a commander.

"Senior Captain Chou," he said calmly, "The Americans are sending a task force to the islands now. They are still out of range for their tilt-rotor troop transports, but they will be in range sometime in the morning. If their plan is to reinforce Taiping, then you do not have the firepower to evict them. So I think it is in all of our best interests if you send the *Jinggan Shan* forward and take that island by morning. Is that understood?"

"Yes, General. I understand and will comply."

General Li handed the handset back to the tech. He would rather have had someone more aggressive in command of the two ships, but Chou was reliable and trustworthy. He would follow orders without question.

He moved back to the plastic chair he had commandeered. It looked like he would be in the command post for the duration. His cell and tablet had been screaming for his attention, so he had finally just turned them off. Evidently, something had leaked out, but if he wasn't at headquarters, he couldn't be questioned.

"General Li, sir," Air Non-commissioned Officer 3rd Class Yan interrupted, calling from his station, "we have some activity from the American task force."

"The carrier group?" he asked as he stood up and walked over to him.

"No General, from the amphibious group."

He pointed to the screen where icons seemed to be lifting off the main icon for the amphibious group.

"These are their Osprey aircraft, General."

General Li looked at their position and calculated distances. They were still too far out, he thought. The tilt-rotor Marine planes had a range of about 1,600 km, and that meant that the planes could not fly to the islands, disembark troops, then return. He wondered if they were only going one way, to land on the island and then stay there. But that would mean that with the three planes that lifted off, there would be somewhere between 72 and about 100 troops sent to Taiping Island, a nuisance, to be sure, but nothing that even the one battalion on the *Jinggan Shan* couldn't handle. He really didn't want the US to get involved with any fighting, but he had always known that the risk of that happening was significant. The Americans had a habit of not considering their best interests before getting involved in the business of others.

He thanked Yan and went back to give Senior Captain Chou the new information. It wouldn't change his mission, but he had to take into account the added US Marines to the ROC Marine forces on the island.

Chapter 10

Over the South China Sea

Major Hayden Cannon looked down at his calculations for the thousandth time. The numbers seemed correct, but as he looked out, he couldn't see a sign of the KC-46 refueler.

They had taken off from the *Makin Island* knowing the distance was too far to take the infantry to Taiping Island and make it back to the ship. And with the comm all screwed up, a normal refueling link-up was out of the question. Mechanically, his Osprey flew fine—it was just that he couldn't communicate with anyone else.

Without satellite navigation he had to use seat-of-the-pants flying, just like pilots back in WWI. At least he could get windspeed from his instruments, so his calculations should be fairly accurate. As a midshipman back at the Academy, he had to learn about set and drift, never in a million years believing that would ever come in handy. But the calculations for flying were essentially the same thing.

He was fairly sure that his flight of four planes was in the right area, but without the tanker, he was going to have to turn back. He could still reach the objective, but he wouldn't have the legs to return. His orders gave him another 15 or 20 minutes to link up with the tanker before he had to abort. Then it would be back to the *Makin Island* to link up with the Osprey that had inserted the recon platoon and wait until the ship got close enough to the objective that they could make the round trip without refueling.

The sun was getting lower on the horizon. Visibility was still good, but it was getting darker. Aerial refueling an Osprey was not particularly difficult, but all things considered, Hayden would rather get the planes refueled while it was still light.

He glanced down one more time at his knee board. Yes, the numbers were correct.

A small red light reflected off of his canopy, just like the movies when a sniper has his victim targeted. He looked off to his left. Off his wing, 1stLt Gravure, the co-pilot for Eight-Seven-Eight, was gesturing, making an exaggerated motion pointing to his left. He had the laser the Navy had given them all, something like a bulked-up laser pointer used for simple lectures and meetings. It had proven pretty effective for catching each other's attention, and they had even been able to send a few simple messages via Morse Code.

Hayden didn't need any Morse Code to know that he and Capt Kranovich had to have spotted the tanker. He pulled his own Osprey up a bit, and sure enough, in the distance, he could see the lights of a large plane.

He began a slow turn to meet the distant plane, the other two Ospreys guiding off of him. He knew the plane had to be the KC-46, but still, he was relieved when they got close enough to confirm that. The tanker had flown from Kadena AFB, so it had to reverse course once the linkup had been made so they would refuel while still closing the distance to the objective.

Although navigating like this was theoretically possible, he hadn't been too confident that they could pull it off, the Ospreys and the tankers coming in from opposite directions and linking up. It had been worth a shot, though, and now it looked that taking that chance would pay off dividends. He would be able to get his PAX on the objective in another hour.

Chapter 11

Beijing

"You tell her that her *Gong Gong* is sorry he missed her party, but that he will bring her something special when he sees her," General Chen told his wife over the phone.

The fact that he missed his granddaughter's birthday party, while not a disaster on a national level, was just one more nail in the coffin of this horrible day. From the opening salvo, he had been scrambling to find answers and assuage everyone from the Politburo on down. To top it off, General Li was still missing, and he needed his deputy chief of staff as a sounding board. Too many of his subordinates told him what they thought he wanted to hear. Li Zhiyuan did not do that. He could be counted on to give an honest and thoughtful opinion.

The Americans, now joined by the Japanese, the Filipinos, and the Russians, were pressing the issue. It was not surprising that the Americans, Japanese, and Filipinos would cooperate in whatever game they were playing. All three were constantly maneuvering to diminish China's power in the region. But now that the Russians were playing, that added a new wrinkle. Either they had been taken in by the American game, or they had their own game in play as well.

General Chen had assured the general secretary no less than four times now that there was no basis to the claims. He was still sure of that even if a few naval units were still out of any communications. That in itself was odd, but it wasn't anything about which to worry.

His secretary announced Major General Guo, head of the Fourth Department, who had called a few minutes ago to say he needed to see him. He told his wife goodbye, assuring her that he would return home when he could, then looked up as Guo centered himself on his desk and saluted. He had a young Air Force captain in tow. The captain looked nervous as he shuffled a folder and his tablet.

"General Chen, I think you need to see something. I didn't want to tell you over the phone, though. This has to be face-to-face."

"Go on," he told Guo calmly, but with a sense of foreboding building up inside of him.

"I would like to turn this over to Captain Xu Da Wu. He is the man who identified this possible anomaly."

General Chen merely nodded as the young man stepped forward. He was clearly nervous, but he spoke with a surprisingly firm and confident voice.

"General Chen Jun, I want to report a problem with our communications systems..." he began before being cut off by the chief of staff.

"A problem with our communications? You are from the Fourth Department. Your mission scope covers enemy communications, not our own."

The captain looked up at his immediate boss, who was avoiding eye contact with anyone.

"Yes General Chen, that is our mission, of course. However, in order to determine if any enemy has penetrated our own systems, we do examine and test them. This is akin to you scanning your home computer or tablet for worms or viruses."

"OK, go on," the general prompted him, not liking the direction in which this conversation was going.

Capt Xu took a deep breath before continuing, "Nothing was evident at first, but I noticed a few anomalies. It's hard to describe them even now, but they were like little dust balls, innocuous, but out of place. That made me look deeper and with more care, and I found what I believe to be some serious breaches in our systems."

"And what do you mean by 'breaches,'" the general asked.

"Sir, I can't say just yet what they are and how they act, but I can say with all certainty that they are there. There are tracks, if I can call them that, all over the place. They have to be doing something, but I just can't tell you what yet."

General Chen felt a rise of elation.

"I knew it! The Americans are behind all of this. I've got to let the general secretary know about this!"

He started to get up when the captain held up a hand to stop him.

"General Chen, I have to inform you that these tracks were not made by the Americans," Xu said quietly.

"Not the Americans? Then who?" he asked in a confused voice.

"I am ashamed to tell you, General, that they were made by us. By the People's Republic of China."

General Chen flopped back into his seat, stunned. Someone in China had manipulated the PLA's computer systems? Was this in-house, possibly a coup? But surely he would be aware if the Army was planning the first coup in the PRC's history. It couldn't be the PLA.

If not the PLA itself, then who?

Then his heart dropped. If it wasn't the PLA, then it had to be the party or the state, not that it mattered as they were one and the same.

He asked Captain Xu to show him the data. He was sure that the captain was correct, though. What he had to figure out now was what to do about it. If this was a party plot of some kind, he needed to determine who were the players and who stood to benefit. Once he knew that, he would then decide what to do to protect the PLA. If that also served to protect him, all the better, but his priorities were to the PLA and to the nation as a whole.

Chapter 12

Aboard the USS Mississippi in the South China Sea

Sergeant Jesus "Jay" McNamara did a final equipment check of his team. They would be the second team to lock out. SSgt Lesean Tolbert's team was already in the lock-out chamber with the lieutenant, and his team was waiting for it to cycle through.

The *Mississippi* was a *Virginia*-class attack sub, and as such, it had the integral lock-out trunk, capable of letting eight divers exit the sub. This was the first time Jay would lock out of an actual trunk. In training he had locked out through a torpedo tube, which was claustrophobic, to say the least. From what he saw in the walkthrough, though, this looked pretty high-speed-low-drag.

The last few hours had been hectic, to say the least. Not just the last few hours, the last day. It was only about 30 hours ago that he had been sitting down at a Pattaya bar to grab a beer and ogle the dancers that the recall had been made. From there the amphibious group had made its mad dash to the South China Sea with the Marines and sailors in frantic planning mode. When the lieutenant had finally given them their op order, they had almost no time to fine-tune anything. They would have to execute and adjust as necessary.

First team was assigned to go with India Company to the Taiwan-held island, leaving Tolbert's Second Team and his own Third Team to go with the lieutenant to the Filipino Thitu Island, what they called Pagasa Island.

Sergeant McNamara was a boot sergeant, perhaps still a little green to be a team leader, but when the shit hit the fan, he was still a Marine and expected to perform like one.

Getting to the sub had been a mission in and of itself. They had boarded one of the Ospreys in the late afternoon, then flew over the water for a couple of hours before somehow finding the *Mississippi* in the middle of nowhere. With the Osprey hovering, they fast-roped down to the rolling deck of the sub. A submarine on the surface is not the most stable platform in the world, and the target portion of the deck was pretty small. One Marine, LCpl Mater actually missed the small flat area and hit the sloping sides of the sub as it rolled, falling into the water. He was immediately fished out by the Navy crew, but it was a reminder that this was the real shit.

Somehow, they all made it aboard along with their gear. The *Mississippi* didn't have a Special Operations Forces Stowage Container, so they had to bring all their own tanks as well as the gear needed for the mission.

While the *Mississippi* steamed (Jay didn't know if "steaming" was the correct term for a nuclear attack sub) to the objective, both teams went over their gear, making sure everything was in top working order. When locking out of a submarine at 70 feet below the surface, it didn't pay to have anything malfunction. They also made good use of the galley. The food was surprisingly good, and they even had ice cream.

The lieutenant and the gunny went over the plan several more times, making some minor modifications. Jay wasn't sure the changes would make any difference given their lack of accurate intel, but they couldn't hurt, he figured. Jay's team was assigned to the main buildings to try and gather information as well as to protect the civilians in case the Chinese decided to take retribution on them once Kilo arrived. SSgt Tolbert's team was assigned to take out the Chinese anti-aircraft battery.

This would not be Jay's first action with some of the members of Kilo. Jay had been with then Lt Niimoto's platoon on the hostage rescue in Somalia, so he had worked with Captain Niimoto, 1stSgt Davidson, Gunny Dailey, Sgt Steptoe, and Sgt Issac. To bring the web even tighter, his platoon commander, Lt Van Slyke, had been with the captain when the skipper won his Navy Cross at New Delhi.

Coincidences were one thing, but from what he had heard, Captain Niimoto liked to surround himself with people he trusted, and he had the pull to get people assigned to him. Jay's own assignment to the recon unit supporting the BLT, though, was most certainly a coincidence.

Jay felt much closer to the first sergeant though, than to the captain. It was the first sergeant, back when he was a staff sergeant, who had run up behind him while out on the *Jason Dunham's* tiny flight deck, urging him to run faster. Jay was a pretty big guy, and it was hot that day. He was about to quit when Davidson, in his black Ranger t-shirt, basically shamed him into pushing it. It wasn't until afterwards that he realized he had it in him to push it, that it felt no worse after pushing it than when he just plodded along.

That had made him run each day he had free time, anxious to see his platoon sergeant, wanting to show him that he was improving. And he felt Davidson had taken him under his wing, almost like a big brother. So when SSgt Davidson had bolted off with Cpl Steptoe back into Hobyo, the Somali city where they had rescued the two hostages, Jay didn't know why he was leaving the safety of the beach, but he knew he had to follow him.

The platoon sergeant had ordered Jay to take back the body of Capt Svenson, so Jay wasn't with him when he found Lt Niimoto and rescued him. But his intent had been to cover Davidson's back, no matter what, and he still felt that way today. There was no expiration date on loyalty.

Without Davidson, Jay probably would not be in recon. It was the enjoyment of running that his platoon sergeant had awakened in him that turned him from a big soft Marine to a big hard Marine, one who naturally gravitated to recon. He had always been at home in the water, and now he had the physical and mental endurance to excel in the unit.

That would probably surprise any of his homeboys back in Flagstaff. Back there, he was still Jesus, the slightly pudgy goth boy. Oh, he had been on his school football team ("Go Eagles!"), but that had been mostly due to his size. He was more at home helping his mother with the taqueria and playing his video games.

If he got his coloring from his mother, he got his size from his father, and it was his father who convinced him to join the Marines.

Not that his father liked the military—in fact it was the complete opposite. To say that Colin McNamara was not the best father around was an understatement. He disappeared for months at a time, showing up for awhile, promising that things would be different this time, and getting a few dollars from his mom before proving that this time was no different.

During the last time he was home, while somewhat drunk, he went on a rant about the military and how it was the tool of an imperialistic and dictatorial government. That perked up his ears. If his dad was against the military, well, maybe that was something for him. So after graduation, with his mom's blessing, he had joined, only expecting to serve one enlistment, then using the GI Bill to get his degree. He never expected that he would like it so much.

And now, here he was, onboard a nuclear submarine, getting ready to walk out of it while it was still 70 feet down. His friends back home would never believe it.

The signal light on the walkout trunk turned green. The first group had already exited and the trunk was ready for them. He sent in LCpl Maus first, then they passed in the tanks before he entered the chamber, to be followed by the rest of his team, the gunny, and Doc Swanson. The trunks were designed for nine men, and with the eight of them and the Navy diver who would work the chamber, it was a tight fit.

The diver (Jay couldn't remember his name) went over the procedures yet again, but Jay was going over the mission again in his mind. He couldn't screw this up.

Everyone put their tanks on and checked their equipment. When each Marine and the doc gave their thumbs up, a sailor outside the trunk closed and locked the hatch. The diver started letting the water in from the outside. Immediately the trunk began to fill and the pressure began to build. This was different than diving down and clearing your ears and sinuses. When diving, you could stop for a moment if you were having a problem clearing. In the trunk, as long as the Navy diver was letting water in, you had to clear on his schedule. But he watched everyone closely. If anyone held out his hand, thumb down, he would stop until that person could clear.

When the water was chest deep, the diver turned off the white lights and turned on the red lights. The top of the sub was 70 feet below the surface, but no use showing any lights to prying eyes.

It was only a minute or two until the trunk was completely flooded. The diver signaled the OK with his forefinger and thumb, then swam up the big metal tube that dominated the top of the trunk. Maus, who was going to be the navigator, followed him. When his fins disappeared, the rest followed in their designated order.

Jay took his turn, swimming up the tube, which looked like nothing more than a cheap chimney. It was big enough, though, to easily fit him, his pack, his weapon, and his tanks. As he exited the hatch, he automatically looked back at the sub, the huge bulk a dark shadow beneath him.

When the gunny joined them, the Navy diver gave them another thumbs up and re-entered the trunk. They were on their own now. Divers are used to hand-and-arm signals, so without too much fanfare, they formed up and began to swim off, LCpl Maus leading the way with his dive board, LCpl Brugal swimming directly over him, scanning the water in front of him.

The water was clear, and in the darkness, plankton lit their passage with an eerie, radioactive-looking glow. Jay held up his hand, watching it become outlined as he disturbed the water with his passage, exciting the plankton. Despite the decent visibility, though, each Marine had a buddy rope connecting him to his swim buddy.

The waters around the Spratlys were pretty deep, especially near the Manila Trench. But most of the islands themselves were protected by coral reefs. Within 30 minutes, they had reached the reef just to the west of the island. He couldn't see it, but Jay knew there was a sunken Filipino Navy ship near them, a victim of that reef.

They eased themselves over the reef, careful not to break the surface of the water and possibly be spotted from shore. Once over, the water deepened a bit, but they could now see the bottom. Jay halted the team, then with PFC Wellington dangling below him on the other end of his buddy line, he and Maus slowly came to the surface. Scanning the beach ahead, he caught sight of a small, faint glow. That was their target. Maus took a bearing on it, and the two slowly sank back down.

With their new bearing, it was only about five minutes before they were more crawling than swimming as they eased ashore. LCpl Mater met them, pocketing the small glowstick he had used to signal them, and led them into the low but dense trees to where the lieutenant was waiting.

First Platoon, Bravo Company, First Reconnaissance Battalion was on enemy-held territory.

Chapter 13
Beijing

General Li looked at the screen, willing somehow that the icons were a glitch, a bug. But he knew they were accurate. There had been three lifts of planes to land on Taiping, and now a fourth was taking off from their amphibious carrier, now less than 300 km away. The first lift had only three planes, with one going off to the south before turning back, but the next two lifts had four planes each. So that meant there could be as many as 360 US Marines on the island to complement the 80 Taiwan Marines already there. That was up to 450 troops to defend it.

He could order the assault now that his own two ships were waiting within an hour's steam of the island. He certainly had enough soldiers to take it in an all-out fight. But the problem was their ability to quickly build up forces. Even though each ship had LCACs, and each ship had helos, none of these were in large enough numbers to be able to get forces ashore quickly enough to overwhelm the defending forces. He thought he could still prevail, but the cost would be high. And with the American planes returning to their task force, they might be able to land even more troops before that bleating lamb of a Senior Captain Chou could get his troops in the assault.

For the hundredth time during the night, he wished he had taken in the Air Force on the plan. One J11 fighter could have quickly knocked the US planes out of the air. But General Li frankly did not have anyone high enough in the Air Force hierarchy that he could trust, and secrecy was paramount until after the islands had been seized. The Air Force tended to be pretty "progressive," a term that merely meant "out-for-oneself" to him, more concerned with economic factors than with national security. So in order to keep the circle of leadership smaller, he had bypassed the Air Force. Only five people currently knew the true scope of the operation and its reason, not including whomever on the Politburo had been pulling his strings. The rest of the actual fighters, from private to senior captain, thought that the Americans were the aggressors and that the entire party and military leadership were coordinating their response. Now, the general was wishing he had brought in at least one more person, someone wearing Air Force blue.

He had to admire the pure balls of the Americans, though. To fly those tilt-rotor aircraft blindly to a refueling point was an ambitious move. He had watched the screen with dismay as the three planes had hooked up with the larger one coming from their base in Okinawa. There was nothing else it could be rather than a refueling link, and when the planes had not only landed but then took off again, it was confirmed.

He wondered if it was time to brief General Chen and the politicians. He had really wanted to already have Taiping in Chinese hands before he did that, but with Thitu Island, maybe that was enough to goad the leadership into taking action. It wasn't as if the Americans were going to meekly slip away. China was going to have to take them down a notch.

On the other hand, maybe he could bring in one Air Force general, one person who could control a few assets. One J11 earlier would have done it, but now, perhaps a few more assets would be required. He hadn't wanted to damage any of the structures on the island, but that might not be an option at this point. At least there weren't any civilians on Taiping, unlike on Thitu. It just all boiled down to timing.

"Mr. Sung, you are positive that enemy communications are still down?"

"Yes, General Li. We remain in full control of all satellites, and there are no sea-cables between the two islands and anywhere else. Of course, as I informed you before, while we are also jamming the immediate area, we do not know if there is an older system available that can be used to slip though our coverage. I can think of three methods myself that could be used to communicate with either ships outside our coverage or with the mainlands of Vietnam or the Philippines."

"And we have no indication that they are certain on what is happening?"

"Other than the fact that they have sent a task force? Well, no, we have collected no SIGINT to that fact, but as you know, we are not fully staffed for that."

The general chose to ignore the slight tinge of sarcasm in Sung's reply. He looked back at the opposition forces screen. The *Gerald R. Ford* battle group had stopped off the coast of Okinawa and was now making square circles in the ocean. It was imperative that they stayed out of any fight-- even if he had the entire resources of the PLA in his hands, he knew that if they waded in, he would have a very difficult time defeating them.

He wasn't sure if it was uncertainty on what was actually happening that kept the battle group away or concern over what had happened to the two Filipino Gripens. General Li thanked his lucky stars that it had been fairly easy for the Second Department to infiltrate Saab, and in routine upgrades, a simple kill switch had been installed in the planes. If it had been the Malaysians who had responded with one of their Russian-made SU-30's, well, despite their nominal efforts to date, those planes were secure from Chinese actions (the Malaysians were just not as high a priority to their efforts.) They might not have been able to communicate, but they could have flown and fought.

The Americans, on the other hand, were perhaps the highest priority. But even with their forces, there were gaps. On the carrier off Okinawa, while the F-35's were all compromised, the older F-18's that had gone through their most recent upgrade were pretty much secure. But as they wouldn't know that, he thought that would keep even the F-18's grounded for the time being.

Based on what he knew, he thought it would take the Americans at least a week or more to analyze their aircraft and take remedial action. He had no doubt that they would figure it out, though, so his window of opportunity was limited.

He yawned and looked at his watch. The city would be coming alive as people started stirring and getting to work. He needed a shower, he knew, and he could use a few hours sleep, but he wondered if he should try and make contact with Lieutenant General Li, the most likely Air Force candidate to go along with the plan. He knew, though, that time was of an essence. He couldn't keep the operation under wraps for much longer—he was somewhat surprised that the veil of secrecy had lasted as long as it had, to be honest.

He stood up to get a cup of tea when the operator on the opposing forces screen motioned to Sung. The general walked back over to see what had caught his attention. Sung saw him come up and stepped aside so the general could see.

The recent flight of aircraft to take off of the American ship was not headed to Taiping. It was heading to Thitu. They were going to try to take it back, it seemed.

The general was glad that he had diverted what was supposed to be the second wave to go to Taiping down to Thitu. It was only another 40 men on the two fishing boats, but when the Taiwan Marines had stood off the first wave, he had not wanted to waste the smaller second wave, so he had sent them to Thitu, mostly just to wait until they were needed. Now, it looked like they might be needed right where they were.

But this was upping the ante. While the Americans might suspect the attack on Taiping was conducted by the Chinese, they couldn't be sure. If somehow they landed their planes on Thitu, and they were not all shot down, confirmation of that would be there.

And confirmation was not what his guardian angel on the Politburo needed. General Li was astute enough to realize that whatever political firestorms were raging, the simple fact that no one on the Politburo "knew" what was happening let them deny, argue, and create doubt amongst their enemies. This is what the Americans termed "plausible deniability," one of the few English phrases he remembered from his classes at the National Defense Academy. The time spent arguing and denying gave him time to complete the mission before presenting it to the world at large.

He wished he had better communications with the small group on Thitu. Communications with the two big ships were fine, but the same cyber-jamming of the opposing communications seemed to be affecting their smaller unit radios. Sung had given him some half-ass excuse as to why there were problems, but the bottom line was that communications were intermittent at best the further any unit went south.

He looked up to Commander Hung, his Navy representative, a man personally picked by his father, Admiral Hung, to assist him.

"Commander, I want you to order Senior Captain Chou to send the *Jinggan Shan* south to Thitu Island and prepare for a landing. Keep the *Changbai Shan* at its present position and await further orders. And keep trying to raise Major Ching on Thitu. He needs to be warned about the incoming assault."

The young commander hurried to comply as General Li Zhiyuan went to the toilet to shave and straighten himself up before going back to the headquarters. He knew he was at a nexus, and he had to take action. Complete secrecy was gone, and now he had to get the other key players in the military and the country at large to not only accept, but embrace the new China era.

Chapter 14
Pagasa Island

"You, empty the bucket," the Chinese soldier told her, pointing at the white paint bucket that was now full of urine.

Analiza sighed inwardly, but let nothing show on her face. This wasn't the first time she had been called to latrine duty.

Just as the Chinese soldiers began their attack, Rayner Umberto, the assistant public works engineer, had shut down the power plant. This wasn't just a simple on and off switch, although such a switch did exist. This was a disguised kill switch that he had shown her once, used to disable the generator in just such an emergency. He had then used an old M16 to fire on the generator, destroying a few cables as a red herring before stashing the weapon and sneaking away to be taken prisoner with the rest of them.

The fighting had been over quickly, but the Filipino soldiers had just given him enough time to get this done. This was not without cost, of course. Taken by surprise with most of them asleep in the barracks, six soldiers had been killed, not including Alan, five had been seriously wounded, and the rest captured. Only one Chinese soldier had been killed in the fighting, although another two seemed to be wounded pretty seriously.

Without power, neither the water pumps nor the desalination station worked. So they had no lights, no running water, no anything. The Chinese had taken Rayner and Val Williams, the chief engineer for the town, to try and fix the generator, but after making a good show of replacing wires and cables, they "failed" in their efforts to get it working. Analiza had been concerned that the Chinese might use more violent ways of getting them to fix it, and she knew that Val would break under the slightest of coercion methods, but the Chinese basically left them alone after they had supposedly tried.

After taking over the island, the Chinese had gathered them all into the community center, posting several armed guards with them at all times. While the surviving soldiers were handcuffed, the civilians were not.

Without working toilets, a large bucket that had been a plaster bucket in a previous life had been surrounded by a sheet to become a makeshift toilet for excrement, and two smaller buckets were for urine. But over two hundred people created a lot of body waste, and the smell could get pretty ripe. So the buckets had to be emptied regularly.

Analiza lifted the bucket, careful to avoid spilling any on either the floor or her legs. The ammonia-smelling vapor made her eyes water, but she made her way to the main door. The soldier who had told her to empty the bucket opened the door for her.

"Not close this time. You take it far, to the trees," he told her, pointing out into the darkness.

He gave her a flashlight, but she wasn't sure how to hold it and the bucket at the same time as it took both hands to heft her load.

Another soldier stood on guard outside the door, and he pointed to the trees as well. None of the soldiers could speak Tagalog or Visaya, as far as she could tell, although she realized that could be a bit of subterfuge. But several did speak English, a few surprisingly well. She nodded to the second soldier, then carefully took the three steps down to the ground.

The bucket handle was digging into her hands, so she put it down for a moment, straightening back up and stretching. Four soldiers were in position around the two sides of the community center that she could see. Another group of half a dozen or so was sitting in front of the general store, seemingly relaxing and chatting. Several broke out into a laugh at something another must have said. She couldn't see any of the rest, but she knew some must be over at the missile launcher they had erected down close to the runway. The starlight and waxing moon was bright enough to let her see what was around her, but the launcher was too far away for that.

Bending back over, she lifted the bucket, splashing a bit over the side and onto her foot. She was tempted to just dump the rest right there on the sparse grass, but she didn't know if the soldier was still watching her.

Overall, the Chinese were treating them as well as could be expected, even letting the town doctor treat the wounded soldiers and Gracie Belvedere, who had somehow taken a round into her thigh during the fighting. But she didn't want to openly defy any of them, giving them the excuse to erupt into the orgy of violence she still expected at any moment.

The open area around the buildings seemed larger when carrying a full bucket of urine. She turned on the flashlight and held it while holding the bucket handle at the same time, sort of straddling the bucket while she duck-walked to the trees. The flashlight helped a bit, but she could not aim it right to where she needed it to see where she would be stepping. She was afraid she would step into a hole, spilling everything over her.

She finally made it to the small, densely packed scrubs they called trees, not that they would deserve that title anywhere back home on Cebu. They were barely 10 feet high this close to town.

Picking the bucket up, she half poured, half threw the contents into the brush. There was something odd about the sound of it though. She did not get the expected splashing sound of urine hitting the leaves both still in the bushes and as ground litter but rather a more subdued sound. She put down the bucket and lifted up the flashlight to look.

At first she could not comprehend what she was seeing. The leaves looked weird, the pattern and color a bit off. And with urine soaking everything, there were dark spots. Then, like a camera coming into focus, her brain registered what she was seeing. A man was lying on the ground. A soldier man, dressed in soldier clothes, goggles over his eyes, and holding a rifle pointing right at her.

Surprisingly, she wasn't frightened. While his face was painted up, this man was not Chinese, nor was he Filipino. In a flash, she realized he had to be an American. The man slowly brought up a finger to his lips, indicating she needed to be quiet.

"But, . . . what . . . ?" she started before shutting her mouth.

He had asked her to be quiet, and here she was talking? She quickly flipped off the flashlight, and he disappeared from her sight. She knew he was in that pool of darkness just a few feet from her, but she could see nothing.

When she heard nothing else, she picked up her bucket and turned back. As she walked her pulse raced. She expected to hear shouts, shots, anything. But there was nothing.

As she climbed back up the stairs and into the community center, she looked around, wishing she could tell someone, anyone what she had seen. But she was wary, not trusting one of the Chinese soldiers to not be able to understand one of the local languages. She felt like she had to do something, though.

She brought back the empty bucket, and on a sudden whim, grabbed the other, even if it was only half full. She picked it up and began to take it outside. The guard looked at her with his eyebrows raised, but said nothing.

As it was only half full, she could carry it across the grass with only one hand. She looked ahead, trying to see just where she had dumped the previous bucket. The tree line was basically featureless.

She got to the trees, trying to perhaps smell the urine, but with the other bucket beside her, she wasn't sure if she was smelling that or the previous load. She couldn't tarry, though, so she bent over and slowly emptied the bucket on the ground.

"There are 206 civilian prisoners in the community center. That's the building that I came out of. There are 15 Filipino soldiers held prisoner there, too, but they are handcuffed. Five are hurt pretty bad. There are close to 60 Chinese soldiers here, all armed with rifles, some kind of small rocket launchers, and a missile launcher down by the runway. At the community center, there are about 15 of the soldiers. I don't know where the rest are. God be with you," she said in a measured, forced whisper.

She was about to straighten up when a voice whispered out from about 5 yards to her right.

"Did you say 60 soldiers? Six-zero? Not 20?"

She paused, before answering back into the bushes, "Sixty. Six-zero. There were about 20 at first, but another 40 arrived yesterday."

She waited for another question, but when none came, she straightened back up and turned around.

As she stepped off to return to the center, a voice whispered out, "Thank you, miss. And God be with you, too."

Chapter 15
Pagasa Island

1stLt Pete Van Slyke motioned to Sgt McNamara to come to him, then waited, feeling the slosh of cold urine soaking through his clothes. None had hit his face, thank goodness, but his utilities and flak jacket had gotten a pretty good soaking.

He had watched the young Filipina make her way right to him, lugging the heavy bucket. They had observed a couple of other buckets being emptied before, but whether that was dishwater, food, or what, they couldn't tell, and the buckets had been dumped much closer to the community center. The girl had been struggling, so the bucket had to have been heavy. She had a flashlight, but the beam was bouncing all over the place, not giving her a good path.

She had kept on walking, getting closer and closer. Night vision goggles were great, but they washed out color and depth. Still, he could tell she was rather attractive and quite petite. Her long hair had kept falling in front of her face, but with two hands holding the bucket and flashlight, she couldn't brush it back. He had a sudden urge to jump out and help her.

She had walked right up to where he was lying. He hadn't wanted to move, but he couldn't help but to shrink back a bit. Then, she had picked up the bucket and threw it into the bushes, most landing right on him. It was piss.

He had automatically raised his rifle, and when she had shone the flashlight on him, he had to will himself to remain calm. The chances were that she was not aligned with the Chinese. She was pretty obviously a Filipina civilian. So he had taken a deep breath, trying not to cough on the ammonia fumes, and had motioned her to be quiet.

She had looked startled and started to say something, but then she had gathered herself and walked back. Pete had hoped she would stay calm and quiet, but he had watched the community center closely for any sign of alarm.

He had glanced over to his right where LCpl Maus was lying. Mau had a smirk visible under his goggles. Pete had to smile, too. He guessed it was pretty funny.

When the girl had appeared again, with another bucket, Pete had perked back up. She had made it back almost to the same spot, then had whispered her message. That had taken him by surprise. There were 60 Chinese on the island, not 20?

He had spotted about 14, and he had figured that there were a few down at the launcher, but where were the other 40? Cpl Holleran and LCpl Brugal were somewhere on the other side of the town, getting eyes on that side, but without comm, they had to make their way back before he would know what they had spotted.

Sgt McNamara crept up to lay beside him.

"Man, sir, that's just not right," he whispered, sniffing at him. "I wondered what she threw at you, and I had my suspicions, but wow!"

"Yea, yea, I know. I know I'll hear about it later, but now, we've got to get a message back to Capt Niimoto. That young lady told me there are 60 Chinese soldiers here, not 20."

"Sixty? Shit!" was the sergeant's response.

"I want you to send two men back to the insertion point and hold up the light board with '60 enemy' on it."

"Aye-aye, sir, but you came through this crap. It's pretty thick, and it'll take them awhile to get there. And if the sub's watching, well, I hope they can relay the message."

"Look, we didn't run across anyone in the bush. It doesn't look like they are running patrols. Probably too secure with whatever cyber-warfare things they've got going. So tell them to stand up and move when they get out of earshot. Grab Pags. He's got the light board. And send someone with him. Tell them to stop back on the other side of town and do what they deem best when the shit hits the fan."

"I'll send DeStafney with him," Sgt McNamara whispered back, then started crawling away.

Pete thought that was a good choice. Cpl Pagano was his comm NCO, a competent Marine in his own right, but Cpl DeStafney was one of the top Marines in the platoon.

Before they left the sub, one of the petty officers had given him a black metal board he had fabricated. After plugging in a keyboard, they could input letters or numbers, 15 characters in all, that lit up on the board. The petty officer assured them it was waterproof, and the boat's XO told him that they would keep a periscope trained on the beach. At their high magnification, they should be able to see any messages.

How they would be able to pass that message on to the MEU was another question. But Pete had to try. Kilo Company needed to know what they faced.

Chapter 16
Pagasa Island

Sgt McNamara looked at his watch for the umpteenth time. Only a minute had passed since the last time he had checked. He grimaced, knowing he needed to calm down.

He was nervous, though. With DeStafney on the other side of the town (he hoped), there were only the five left from his team, Doc Swanson, and the lieutenant here. Their mission was not to take out the Chinese forces—that was the job of Kilo Company. Their mission was to protect the civilians while SSgt Tolbert's team was to take out the missile battery. But with over 60 Chinese soldiers in a defensive posture, that would be a tougher nut to crack for Capt Niimoto.

At least Holleran had located the bulk of the Chinese. He had gotten back only 30 minutes before and reported that the soldiers had seemed to be bedding down at what was designated as the mayor's house on their map.

While their mission was protecting the civilians, the lieutenant, still stinking of piss, had told him that given the opportunity, they would help even the odds somewhat for Kilo. Of course, that left them up shit creek without a paddle if things went south. So the more they did for Kilo, the faster Kilo could take back the island and keep the Chinese off of the platoon's ass.

He looked at his watch one more time. *Crap! Only another minute gone.*

As the sun started making its presence known in the east, there had been a small degree of stirring around the town. One soldier had walked out towards the runway, smoking a cigarette. He stopped before reaching it, though, and stood there in the open area, scratching his balls with one hand and controlling the cigarette with the other. He wasn't that far from Jay, so he could clearly see the soldier holding the butt with his thumb and forefinger, the other three fingers splayed up, in an OK-kind of position.

Jay wasn't sure why the assault wasn't going to be done in the wee hours of the morning under the cover of darkness. It didn't seem like a good idea to let the Chinese wake up and get their heads on straight before the attack.

Jay was more nervous now than he had been in Somalia, even if that had been his first taste of combat. In Somalia, he had been a PFC, just following orders. He had been a bit scared, but in his heart, he really didn't think he could actually die. Carrying Capt Svenson's body back had made it sink home a bit, but he had been off the beach shortly after that.

Now, as a sergeant, he felt the responsibility for his team. It wasn't just Joe-grunt Jesus McNamara worrying about what he had to do, it was Recon Team Leader Jay McNamara worrying about what everyone was supposed to do. He was afraid of failure more than of personal injury.

He looked at his watch again. At last! Within a minute, SSgt Tolbert would take out the missile battery. And if all went according to plan, about four minutes later, Kilo would land.

Jay crossed himself, then took out the small wooden crucifix that hung around his neck and kissed it. He felt more than saw a stirring as the other Marines around him got ready for action.

Even though he was expecting it, when he heard the firing open up not 400 meters away, he flinched. He couldn't see the missile battery through the trees on the other side of the opening leading to the runway, but he could see the smoker who startled, swung around to look in the direction of the battery, then started running back. He hadn't even brought his weapon with him.

They withheld their fire as the soldier ran back into town. There was no use in firing on him and giving out their position just yet. The gunfire at the battery intensified for a moment, then there was an explosion. Smoke started to rise over the trees. First Team had connected.

The guards at the community center ran to the south side of the building to look. This was poor tactics. If the Marines had wanted to attack the building, having the guards now all on one side left three sides undefended. Evidently another Chinese soldier saw that, too, because he came running up, yelling at the bunched-up guards. The guards split up, going back to their previous posts.

The firing stopped. Jay wondered if that signaled success or if Tolbert's team had been taken out. As Chinese soldiers rushed into view, a much larger blast echoed, and Jay could see a huge metal part from the battery rise up 100 or 150 feet, tumbling end over end. That pretty much sealed the deal. Green smoke puffed up to join the black billowing skyward—green was the color to signal the Ospreys. That done, SSgt Tolbert would be moving back towards the town, keeping in the trees, though, so they wouldn't be able to move quickly.

Jay strained to hear the sounds of the approaching Ospreys. They could not afford to have been close enough to be within range of the battery before it was taken out, but now, it was imperative that they land before the alerted Chinese could better prepare for them.

About a dozen soldiers rushed from the direction of the mayor's house and ran into the community center. Jay tensed up. If the Chinese blamed the Filipinos for some home-grown sabotage, then they would have to move quickly to keep them from suffering reprisals.

Several of the soldiers came back out with one of the Filipino men and seemed to be questioning him. Jay sighted in on the soldier who looked like he was in charge, waiting to take the shot if need be. But while the Filipino looked uncomfortable, he didn't seem to be being threatened, merely questioned.

Then he heard it. The Osprey was a big bird, but it could move quickly, so from the time that it could be heard until it arrived was generally somewhat short. Away from the town, back towards the north end of the island, the Osprey was rapidly making its approach.

Jay couldn't see it, and neither could the soldiers on the front porch to the community center, but they could all hear the plane.

The plan was for the first plane to come in low and fast-rope its Marines right into the dense tropical scrub about 600 meters north of the town. This would keep the bird out of direct fire from anyone on the ground except for possibly from the far southern end of the island, but that would be a pretty long shot, and hopefully, SSgt Tolbert's team would have eliminated that threat.

This insertion should focus the Chinese attention towards the north when the next three birds would come in at wave height, essentially dropping their ramps right on the runway, doing a slow taxi while the Marines jumped out. With the Chinese attention towards the north and the three Ospreys using the trees along the north side of the runway as cover, hopefully, the Marines could debark and the Ospreys could get back into the air to provide supporting fire.

One of the problems with the Osprey was that it was faster and had longer legs than anything else in the MEU. Cobra II's could not provide air support, and with the fast movers grounded, the Ospreys had to provide their own support.

There was a mad flurry of activity as officers or NCO's started giving orders and the rush of Chinese soldiers started to organize into recognizable tactics. Jay was disappointed, though, when a good dozen or so soldiers who were in view oriented to the south, and among them was a heavy machine gun. Whoever was in charge there was not an idiot.

Jay looked over at PFC Wellington, pointing to the machine gun, maybe 300 meters away. Wellington nodded. That would be their target.

The Osprey to the north could still be heard when the faint addition of the ones coming in to the south became noticeable. Jay was listening for it, so he heard it first, but after only a few moments, the Chinese became more focused. They had picked up on it, too.

With the southern part of the island so flat, visibility was limited anywhere through the trees, so neither Jay nor the Chinese could see the incoming birds. It looked like the Chinese were orienting down the open area towards the runway, which made sense as the brush was so dense as to make passage extremely difficult.

But the Ospreys never broke past the edge of the trees. If the runway was the top of a T, the open area leading to the town was the lower stem of the T. The Ospreys went down the west end of the T, then did a U-turn and took off again, never coming into the heavy machine gun's sights. But the Marines who had been on those Ospreys would be in view momentarily.

As the six recon Marines and Doc were on the east side of the open area, they would be able to see the Marines just before the Chinese could. And the moment Jay saw that first Marine bounding forward, he opened fire on the machine gun. Within seconds, the rest of them opened up as well.

Three hundred meters across an open, flat area was not particularly far, but it seemed as if their rounds were bouncing everywhere except on target. The Chinese soldiers wheeled around to fire at them, and the machine gunner started to turn his gun around when he slumped. Another soldier pushed him out of the way and started firing, the heavy rounds cutting through the bushes just a foot or so above the recon Marines' heads.

It looked like two rounds impacted the soldier simultaneously, and the heavy gun went quiet. The other soldiers backed away taking cover behind a small white building. Five of them were left motionless on the ground where they had been hit.

Kilo Company Marines were pouring around the edge of the corner in the tree line, rushing forward, covering each other. They were in a kill zone, and the best way to get through it was to move quickly. One of the Ospreys made a long turn out over the sea and started a run in. With the civilians intermixed with the Chinese, it might be limited in where it could fire, but any added support was welcomed.

Recon had taken out the missile battery and a machine gun. Now Kilo Company was in the attack.

Chapter 17
Pagasa Island

Sgt Harrington Steptoe followed in trace of Capt Niimoto. As soon as they had landed, he had tried the comm, but as expected, whatever was jamming them still worked. So he was down to Plan B. Three junior Marines, PFC's Bouchard and Toti and Pvt Sullivan, in turn followed him in trace.

As the company comm chief, he had to ensure there were some means of communications. With normal comm being jammed, he had to reach back to WWI tactics and employ runners and wire. As runners, the young Marines would carry messages back and forth as the skipper required. Once they got in a static position, then the wire would come into play. The *Makin Island* and provided the wire as well as the hand-held phones.

"Come on, Toti, keep it tight," he admonished the slightly-built Marine.

Toti seemed to jump each time rounds went off, and Steptoe wondered if he was the right man for the job. There was nothing that could be done about that at the moment, though.

This was Steptoe's third taste of combat. He had been with the skipper back in New Delhi, then with him again in Somalia. This was his first experience against an actual professional foe, but as before, he had a surprising lack of fear. He wasn't sure why this was. A rational man would have a degree of fear, or at least apprehension. Steptoe really didn't have any.

No one who knew the young Harrington Steptoe would ever have guessed he would end up being a Marine, much less an NCO. While tall for his age, he had always had a degree of softness about him. His father, an accountant, had moved the family when Steptoe was a young boy from Willingboro, New Jersey to Winsted,

Connecticut where they were the only African-American family in the neighborhood and one of the few in the entire town.

On his first day at school, Mr. Martin, the PE teacher had made him one of the captains of that day's basketball teams, and rather obvious case of racial profiling, but Steptoe was able to immediately dispel the idea that all blacks were somehow experts in b-ball with an extraordinary display of a lack of coordination. Steptoe was not a jock. However, the lack of physical coordination he displayed in sports did not follow through on a Wii or Playstation. As a gamer, Steptoe became quite skilled and even took a second place finish at an All-New England Battlefield 4 tournament.

Steptoe was not sure what made him sign up for the Marines. He had seen an old advertisement for the Corps on YouTube, one that made the subject Marine look like he was in a video game, and that had caught his interest. But while on a trip to New York for a tournament (in which he bombed out early), he wandered into the recruiting station and at the spur of the moment, signed up.

At boot camp, he had done quite well in the course work, even if he wasn't the fastest runner or the quickest over the obstacle course. With a first name of Harrington, he was ripe for a nickname. He wasn't happy with the one he received: "Cracker." With his lighter skin and splash of freckles across his nose, his partiality to country western music, and his love of gaming, the other African-Americans had jerked his chain about him not really being black. That hurt him more than he let on, but thankfully, that nickname had fallen out of use by the time he was with his second duty station, New Delhi. There, because of his rather obvious hero-worship of SSgt Child, he gained the new nickname of Stepchild.

That nickname was only used by a few people now, those who had survived the embassy takeover. No new nickname had stuck, and with his formal-sounding first name, he was either Steptoe or Sgt Steptoe, depending on who was addressing him.

Captain Niimoto got up from his kneeling position and ran 10 or 15 meters down the edge of the tree line, so Steptoe got up to follow, motioning for his shadows to get up and move as well. Up ahead, 2d Platoon was in contact, but with the dense brush and trees alongside the opening leading into town, the headquarters element had to stay at the edge the open area as well, out of direct sight from a good portion of the buildings in the town. This still left them vulnerable to fire, either aimed at them or that aimed at the Marines in Second.

One of the Ospreys flew overhead, its Gau-17 minigun letting loose a burst. It swung back to return to the runway area, probably to make another run.

One of the machine gun teams attached to Second was laying a base of fire into the town itself. Steptoe was only a hundred meters or so back, but he couldn't yet see the target. From the return fire, though, it sure seemed like there were more than just 20 Chinese soldiers on the island. They had seen five dead soldiers around the destroyed anti-aircraft battery, so that would have left only 15 or 16 in the town.

He could see firing coming out of the tree line on the east side of the open area, but the small yellow ribbon tied to the top of one of the stunted trees was the signal that this was the recon unit. Steptoe wanted to send a runner over to them to find out what they knew about the enemy, but ordering one of his runners across 200 meters of open area while it was under fire was asking a bit much.

A Marine from Second, Cpl Ayala, it looked like, was hugging the tree line, leading a recon Marine. They spotted the skipper and made a last sprint to flop down beside him. Steptoe edged forward.

"Sir, Cpl Kinney from recon here. We took some friendly fire from your platoon coming in through the trees. We popped the smoke to get them to quit firing us up, but I think that gave away your position to the Chinks . . . oh sorry sir, I mean the Chinese."

"Shit," the skipper replied, seemingly oblivious to the slur. "Anyone hit?"

"Yes sir, LCpl Mater. He's pretty fucked up, but one of your docs is hooking him up now," came the reply.

A flurry of rounds hit the dirt not 2 meters to their right.

"Here, get in here for a moment," Capt Niimoto ordered, and the two Marines, Steptoe, and the three runners wormed their way into the dense brush where they could at least sit up and look each other in the eyes.

Steptoe knew what the skipper was thinking. With 1st Platoon out to the north, making themselves a target of sorts, he had hoped that the Chinese in the town wouldn't know which way to turn when Second began its rush to get into position. But if smoke was popped in the dense brush, that would give away 3d Platoon's position, coming in from the southwest. The Chinese would now know from where their point of main effort was assaulting.

"OK, we're still on track. There were five dead soldiers back on that battery. Your work, I presume?" he asked the recon Marine, who nodded back. "OK, good job on that. Cpl Ayala, what were you able to see in front of you?"

"Well, sir, there were another five KIA's around a machine gun, but they were dead by the time we got up there. And we've been firing back at some others, but I don't know if we hit anyone yet."

"Well, that means there can only be 10 or so soldiers left. We're OK."

"Sir, didn't you get the message?" asked the recon corporal.

"What message?"

He looked to Steptoe out of habit, but without any working comm, Steptoe was just as much in the dark as he was.

"There're around 60 Chinese on the island. We signaled that back to the sub."

"We never got that," the skipper told him as he leaned back, eyes not focusing on anything as he thought.

He came to a decision.

"Where's your lieutenant?" he asked Cpl Kinney.

"Over there, sir," he replied, pointing across the open area to the east tree line.

"OK, who's your team leader?"

"That would be Staff Sergeant Tolbert, sir. But we've also got Gunny Sloan with us."

"You do? OK, then, I want to see the gunny here. Stepchild," he said, turning towards his comm chief.

Capt Niimoto rarely called him by that nickname in public, but old habits had a way of surfacing when stress levels were high.

"I want your runners to get me the platoon commanders for Second and Third, the XO, and Weapons. I don't know if we can get to 1st Platoon and the first sergeant, but I want to try. Then, can you run wire around the perimeter of the town? Inside the tree line?"

Sgt Steptoe looked down at the aerial photo he had been carrying, slowly calculating. It would be close.

"I think I can sir, but it'll take awhile. We have to make our way through this stuff here," he told him, indicating the dense vegetation.

"OK, get on it then. Shanghai whoever you need. Just get it done. And tell the runner you're sending to First that feints and subterfuge are over. They know where we are now. I want that platoon up and in position on the north side. Don't engage unless they're fired upon, but I want to coordinate this better.

"Gunny," he said to GySgt Dailey, who had crept up to join him. "Get some bodies in here and clear this out a bit. I need to be able to talk to everyone. But be subtle. The Chinese have to be watching, so let's not give us away.

"OK, then, let's get to it."

Chapter 18
Beijing

General Li stopped inside the rest room to check himself in the mirror. He looked liked he had been up all night, which was pretty much the case. His meeting with General Li Huang-fu, the Air Force chief of staff, had not gone well. The Air Force General Li had flatly turned him down.

General Li didn't know if that was because the other General Li truly didn't have the vision to see how important this was to China, if he just didn't have the balls to do anything on his own or if this was part of the growing rivalry between the two branches of the PLA. For years the Air Force had been the weaker sister in the armed forces, but over the last decade or so, it had been increasing in political clout. The Air Force General Li might be seeing this as an opportunity to further his service's position, putting politics above the needs of the country.

At least that meeting had forced the general's hand. He now had to bring General Chen into the loop. He wished he knew who exactly on the Politburo was in back of all of this. That would help with Chen. Regardless, he needed more assets to bring the plan to fruition, and at this stage of the game, that meant getting more people involved.

While he had considered the possibility that the Americans would get involved, he was still surprised at the speed in which they had gotten troops on Taiping and were actually assaulting Thitu. He had hopes that Major Ching could hold out, even if the Americans got a foothold on the island. That would give him more leverage.

He had thought the Americans would not risk an all-out war over the islands. Their politicians were no different than those in China, afraid to take action and more inclined to talk, talk, talk.

They hadn't committed their carrier battle group nor their Air Force assets, whether because of fear of the cyber-infection that pervaded their war machines or because doing so could trigger a full-scale war neither country wanted, Li didn't know. The troops they had committed, though, were bad enough, and before he could order another assault on Taiping, he had to have some air assets.

He straightened his tunic, then turned around and walked out. It was time. He knew his presence back at the headquarters would have been reported back to General Chen, so there was no use delaying. Besides, he wasn't a man who waited. He was a man of action.

"General Li," shouted one of Chen's aides, waiting outside the chief of staff's office, "General Chen wants to see you right away! Please come with me."

The general didn't respond to the aide, but he did follow the man. Normally, the general took pains to acknowledge subordinates, but in this case, he needed to project himself in a position of power, of authority.

The bustle of activity in the outer office stopped momentarily as he walked through, all eyes on him. No one there could really know what was going on, but his absence for the last two days had to have created a stir.

General Chen's secretary jumped up, choosing to announce Li's arrival in person rather than over the intercom.

"General Chen, General Li is here to see you," she said as she opened the door to Chen's office.

General Li didn't wait for a response but brushed past her and entered the large and well-appointed office. General Chen had been meeting with Colonel Ho, one of his protégés. The chief of staff looked up with an expression that showed both annoyance and relief.

"General Li, where have you been? I have needed you here, but you disappeared and have been out of communications. I assume you know what's been happening?"

Li inclined his head towards the colonel. General Chen shrugged his shoulders and dismissed him, leaving only the two generals in the room.

Once they were alone, General Chen asked, "You have heard that the Americans, Japanese, Filipinos--just about everybody has accused us of launching an invasion of the Wanli Shitang?"

Li nodded.

"Well, what you don't know, since you have absented yourself, is that this might be true. I have seen evidence that someone has manipulated our own communications and data records. I have the Fourth Department working to unravel it, but evidence points to the possibility that units within the PLA might have taken the opportunity to seize Taiping Island."

"Yes, I am aware of all of that, and you are correct."

Emotions warred on General Chen's face as he digested that. Li could see anger rising, but being pushed back down, if with an effort.

"Your attitude confirms what I feared. At first your absence was an annoyance. I needed you here. But when it stretched through to today, I wondered if you might have some inside knowledge. It had to be you or General Hing. Only you two were really in position to pull something like this off."

Hing? He thought. The commander of the Southern District didn't have the fortitude to act with this degree of conviction.

"So tell, me, why I should not have you arrested right now."

"I think you know why. I am merely a tool in this. I am not acting alone."

"So this is not a coup?" General Chen asked, relief obvious in his voice.

"A coup? Against my own country? Against the party leadership? I think you underestimate my loyalty," was the measured response.

"So if not a coup, then who ordered this?"

"At the moment, I am not at liberty to reveal that."

He would have revealed it, had he only known just who he or they were. Instead, he had to bluff.

General Chen looked down at his desk for a moment before looking back up at the still standing Li.

"So this is being kept from me?"

General Li had anticipated the question, so he had a ready answer.

"It has been decided to keep you clean, in case events did not work out as planned. Someone would have to take the fall, of course, and you were deemed too valuable to the nation. You would be left with cleaning up the mess."

He could see the emotions warring on the chief of staff's face. For someone who had risen to the top of the Chinese military, he sure lacked a poker face. General Chen obviously wanted to believe what he had told him. Anything else meant that he was merely a figurehead, something Li knew to be unpalatable to him.

The chief of staff was silent for a moment before responding.

"And now?" came the unspoken question.

"Now, General Chen, events have transpired so that more resources will be needed to finish the task at hand. What you may not know is that not only have the Americans been going through diplomatic channels to address this, but they have landed troops in opposition to us."

Once again, the chief of staff was silent for a moment as he digested this.

"We are at war with the Americans now?"

"'War' is a very strong term, general. We have come into 'contact' with the Americans, just as we have come into 'contact' with the renegade Chinese on Taiwan, with Japan, India, South Korea, Vietnam...I don't need to lecture you, more than anyone else, of our PLA's glorious history."

"So what is the situation now? How involved is our 'contact?'" he asked.

"The renegade Chinese put up a spirited defense of Taiping. Our assault force never made it to the island. The Americans were able to reinforce it with what is probably a company-size unit. On Thitu, our assault force was able to take the island easily and is in control; however, we believe another American company-size unit may have landed on the island."

"You 'believe?'"

"Unfortunately, the same measures we took to blanket the area has had unforeseen effects on our own communications."

"And how could the Taiwanese troops repel our forces there? They don't have more than 80 or so Marines on the island, if I recall correctly."

"A decision had been made that the assault forces remain limited to ensure secrecy."

He didn't mention that that decision had been his.

"On Thitu, only 20 soldiers took the island, although they have been reinforced with another 40. We had 100 in the assault on Taiping, and 20 took West York Island from the Filipinos. We have another 1,800 afloat and getting in position."

"And...?" General Chen prompted.

"We believe now is the time to dedicate more assets to the assault. We need air assets most of all. The Americans seem to be withholding their carrier battle group and their long-range assets from their air base in Guam. Their opposition looks to be a surgical attempt to get their troops committed, to make us pause."

"Well, maybe we should 'pause,' as you put it."

General Li was afraid of this. The chief of staff was a canny player. He had to be in order to have risen to the top. He would want to get more details before committing himself. He had to see the possibility of glory, but he also realized failure was an option that no military leader, no government or party leader, for that matter, would want to contemplate.

"I am a military man, general. My job, as is yours, is to ensure the People's Liberation Army succeeds in all tasks. As far as pausing, that is up to those on the Politburo who are pulling our strings. But until they should so decide, it is our duty to strive for success. And to achieve success, I believe we need air assets. We have the ground troops in place."

General Chen stood up and walked to the window, looking out over the bustling city. He clasped his hands behind him, then rocked up and down on his heels.

Turning around, he asked, "And why are you coming to me? Why not your superiors, our superiors, on the Politburo and the CMC?"

"I can't answer that. They have their own agenda with aspects far beyond the mere military perspective."

General Li watched the emotions play over the chief of staff's face again. The man was an open book!

Finally, he walked back to his desk, hitting the intercom.

"I want a general staff meeting in 30 minutes," he abruptly instructed his secretary.

To General Li he said, "Before they come, I want a more detailed brief on the situation. If we are going to jump in, then we need to do this right."

General Li felt a rush of relief replacing the tension he hadn't really realized he was feeling. The chief of staff had not committed anything, but neither had he ordered his arrest. All of this could still be salvaged.

Chapter 19

Pagasa Island

There was a sharp crack of shattered leaves followed by the almost simultaneous deadened thud of the round hitting flesh. LCpl Kenny shouted out, sitting up and grabbing his thigh. Sgt Steptoe lunged forward and pulled him back prone.

The Chinese soldiers had taken to putting random shots into the foliage. They had to know something was up as no all-out assault had materialized. And as the amount of wire they had was limited, he could not go too deep into the jungle, so the firing had forced his small group to basically low crawl through the bushes. He had been grateful for this flak jacket, but the various branches had already cut up his hands, his neck, and his legs.

But now a random round had impacted on Kenny's thigh, and blood was spurting out. He kept trying to sit up, but that would expose him to more fire, so Steptoe physically laid on him, hands trying to apply pressure to the thigh.

"Sullivan," he told the private, "go deeper into this by five yards, then get up and get the doc. He needs to get here quick."

Pvt Sullivan nodded, then moved off. Sgt Steptoe looked back at LCpl Kenny, who had gotten pale and was obviously going into shock.

"OK Kenny, hang in there. Doc's coming now. You're going to be fine."

LCpl Kenny stopped trying to sit up, his breath becoming shallow. Blood was pooling under him despite the pressure Sgt Steptoe was putting directly over the wound. He tried to put more pressure, knowing he had to stop the bleeding. Another round cracked through the foliage, but it barely registered on him as Kenny's blood continued to flow between his fingers.

"Toti, help me put pressure here!" he called out.

Pvt Toti looked pale as he crawled up, then hesitantly put his hands on LCpl Kenny's leg.

"Harder, Toti! We need to stop the bleeding!"

LCpl Kenny stopped his mumbling. Steptoe looked up to see him staring upwards, mouth open, small gasps the only sign that he was still breathing.

If doc was there, he knew he could reach inside and clamp or stop the femoral artery from bleeding, but Steptoe didn't know if he could do that. He took pressure off for a moment to see if he could even see the artery, but the bleeding increased, so he pushed back down.

He looked back over his shoulder. *What was keeping Sullivan and the doc?*

Time dragged on. He wanted to look at his watch, to check the time, but he didn't want to let up on the pressure. His arms started to ache with the effort, and Toto was tiring, but they had to keep Kenny alive until doc got there.

"Hey, I think its working!" he exclaimed as the bleeding finally seemed to stop.

He looked up to Kenny's face, and his heart sank. There was no movement, no rise and fall of his chest. LCpl Kenny had bled out.

"OK, Toti, that's enough," he said, bitterness in his voice.

He didn't really know LCpl Kenny very well. He had just grabbed him, "Shanghaied" him, as the skipper had directed him. And because of that, Kenny was dead. Because of his choice. Not the skipper. Not Lt Gaines, Kenny's platoon commander. Sgt Harrison Steptoe. His decision.

He looked at his watch. He had 20 more minutes to get the wire laid.

"OK, let's move out. We need to get this done, but keep your heads down!" he told his small working party.

"What about him?" Pvt Toti asked.

"Leave him here for now. We'll recover him later. Now, we need to get this wire laid."

He couldn't help but to look back and LCpl Kenny's still form as they crawled further into the bush, dragging the wire behind.

Chapter 20
Pagasa Island

Joselito toddled up to Analiza, hands out, offering her his plastic action figure.

"You can play with him, if you want," he told her.

Analiza laughed and gave him a hug despite the situation. Joselito had obviously felt the tension, and this was his way of trying to deal with it. She took the beat up toy.

"Why thank you, Joselito. Maybe you can show me how to play with him?"

She looked around the room as the young boy happily went over the various functions of the plastic figure. All of the Filipinos were there in the middle of the community center, sitting on the floor. Four Chinese soldiers where in there as well, but none of them had made any aggressive moves.

An hour earlier, rounds had hit the center, shattering one of the windows and sending people screaming as they dove for the floor. Since then, however, the firing had died off, although they could still hear some shots being fired sporadically. Analiza wondered what was happening. The four soldiers didn't seem too concerned. It seemed to her that if the Americans were going to rescue them, they would have already done so. Was it possible that the American she had seen was only part of a small force, merely sent to see what was going on?

After the initial firing broke out, a few of the men had been surreptitiously gathering in small groups, whispering together. Whatever it was that they planned, it had to be obvious that the guards could see what was going on. Only four guards or not, they were armed and none of the Filipinos were. Analiza hoped that no one was planning anything foolish.

She glanced up as another burst of fire sounded off in the distance. Whatever was going to happen, she just wished it would happen soon.

Chapter 21
Pagasa Island

"Roger that," 1stLt Peter Van Slyke said over the hand-held phone. "Most of the Chinese seem to be concentrated in the government building in the north and in the adjoining buildings. There're only a couple of soldiers back in the community center with the hostages. My take on it is that they don't want the hostages caught in a crossfire, over."

Peter had been surprised when a Marine had come through the undergrowth with the phone and trailing wire. With all the modern comm gear available to them, it seemed odd speaking into what was essentially an old fashion telephone. It was set up as a party line, for all practical purposes, so getting walked on was a problem. Proper radio procedures were a must.

"Any numbers and disposition of the Chinese, over?" Capt Niimoto's voice came over the phone.

"Movement has been limited, and we can see signs that they're fortifying their positions. But as far as numbers go, it's hard to tell. I'd say at least 25, two-five, soldiers in the government building, maybe 10 or so in the house directly to the east of that, and several more groups of 4 to 5 in the surrounding buildings. On top of the public works building, we think there is either an observation team or a sniper team, over."

"Can you take the sniper team under fire when we begin the assault, over?"

"I'm not sure. If they orient to the north, they will be in defilade towards us. If they orient to the south, then we should be able to take them under fire. I would suggest using the 60's. We're pretty sure there're no friendlies at the location, over."

"Roger, wait one..." the captain said.

Pete raised his binos again to glass the area. Captain Niimoto wanted him to provide a base of fire from the east to help cover the main assault from the north and west. The main base of fire would come from his Second Platoon from the south, but Pete's platoon would be more judicious, taking out whatever target of opportunity presented itself. His Marines would have to be more careful as Third Platoon would be in their line of fire as they moved in on the assault.

He reached down to scratch the welt that was forming on his thigh. Something had crawled in while he was laying there and taken a bite off of him, and the itch was getting maddening. He had been in the same spot for close to eight hours, and what with the bugs and a bucket of piss being thrown on him, comfort was pretty much out the window. He would be glad when things kicked off and he could at least move from this position.

The lack of activity seemed surreal to him. There were five dead soldiers in sight, lying in the sun. There was sporadic harassment fire coming from the Chinese. But after that first flurry of fighting, things went into a hiatus, sort of a Mexican standoff. Pete might not have stalled the attack had he been in charge, but he guessed Capt Niimoto wanted to make sure the assault hit with maximum power. Pete understood that, but the delay also gave the Chinese time to prepare better.

"Second, I want you to send a runner back to the 60's. I want rounds on the roof of the utility building in exactly 25 minutes from my mark. I want an Osprey in the air to follow up with anyone left on the roof. When the mortar rounds impact, that will be the signal to commence the assault. We will stick with white smoke to cease fire as previously planned. Now, I want confirmation, starting with First, over," Capt Niimoto said over the landline.

Pete hadn't seen any sign of an Osprey for at least 30 minutes, so he had assumed they were refueling or something. It was a nice security blanket to know that at least one was on hand.

"First, roger, over."

"Second Platoon, roger, over," was followed by Third Platoon's acknowledgment.

"Recon, roger, over," Pete transmitted.

It seemed odd not to have call signs, but without real comm, things were being kept simple. Of course with wire, it was possible that the Chinese had somehow discovered it, spliced into it, and were now listening in.

"Roger, so everyone's on board. Let's get this thing done. On my mark—five, four, three, two one, mark!"

Pete set his watch, then slowly moved over to Sgt McNamara.

"OK, here it is. In 25 minutes, the 60's will hit the utilities building. That will signal the attack. We're providing the base of fire, but for God's sake, we've got Kilo's Third Platoon right in our line of fire. We need to make sure we target each shot, no un-aimed rounds downrange. And we need to keep our heads low. We don't need any friendly-fire casualties here, either. I want Brugal to target the team on the roof. If the mortars don't get them, if the Osprey doesn't get them, he needs to take them out."

"He'll take them, no problem, sir. What about Gunny Sloan and Staff Sergeant Tolbert? Are they coming back here?" the team leader asked.

"No, it's just us here. Tolbert's team is joining Second Platoon for the base of fire and to act as a reaction force, if needed."

Sgt McNamara nodded, then crawled off to tell the others.

Pete resisted the urge to shout as another creepy crawler decided to sample his thigh, this time dangerously close to his balls. He reached in, felt the little bugger, then pulled it out. His fingers had partially crushed it, but a reddish ant seemed to stare defiantly at him. He flicked it away.

Pete realized that they could be at the brink of WWIII. The Marines were about to conduct an all-out assault on Chinese soldiers. Yet the world went on. Ants scurried in the brush, looking for food, living life as they had done for millions of years. They had bitten dinosaurs, and now they had bitten him. If this was WWIII, they probably would outlast humans, too.

He looked at his watch. It would all kick off in about 15 minutes. This is what he had been trained for, what the US taxpayers paid him to do. The situation might be different than anyone would have guessed. They had none of the modern technology with which he had been trained, none of the comm, not even the heads-up displays in their helmet faceshields. But when you got down to it, combat was combat, man against man. It had been this way since humans first stood upright on the plains of Africa.

He could feel his pulse pounding. He wasn't going to be kicking in doors. He and his team were probably pretty safe as a base of fire unless there were more Chinese on the island than they thought. But he still had a degree of nervousness. He wiped the sweaty palms of his hands on his trousers.

A soldier looked out the door of the government building, then ran full out, changing direction several times as he made it to the adjoining building. No one fired on him, letting him make it safely. Pete wondered what was his mission, why he had to go to the other building. He wondered if the Chinese had the same comm problems that the Marines had. He wondered what the Chinese had done to prepare for the coming fight.

Wondering, though, was not doing any good. He would find out soon enough.

He tried to control his breathing, to calm himself. He had a job to do, and he was going to get it done right.

Time seemed to crawl, yet when he finally heard the soft thunk in the distance of outgoing mortar rounds, it suddenly seemed as if it was too soon, that it should take longer. He counted down the seconds, waiting for the impact.

Even though he was expecting them, he still jumped when the six mortar rounds, two rounds for each tube, impacted all around the utilities building. None landed on top of the building, though, best he could tell. But as firing commenced all around them, an Osprey made its run, its minigun opening up on the rooftop. Dust and pieces of the building went flying. The big bird continued to the north and out of sight.

Marines came into view from the north, rushing out of the tree line. Fire started coming out to greet them, but scan as he might, Pete could not acquire a target. He wasn't sure if Second Platoon had targets in sight, but they were opening up with their small arms, and chips were flying off the southern walls of the buildings.

The muzzle of a machine gun poked out of a window opening and started to fire in the direction of Second, so Pete fired at it. His angle was wrong, though, and he couldn't get at the shooter. More American rounds impacted around the window, and the machine gun disappeared.

A Marine rushing from the north went down, and the single crack of the Chinese rifle seemed clear over the rest of the cacophony of firing. Despite the Osprey, at least one of the Chinese sniper team must have survived.

"Brugal! Take out the sniper!" he shouted, the time for stealth gone.

"Can't see him, sir!" LCpl Brugal shouted back.

"Get to where you can see him, then!"

To his right, a Marine got up and rushed out of the comparative safety of the tree line. It was Sgt McNamara, rushing over the 150 meters or so to the building. Rounds started whistling into the trees as he ran—their fellow Marines were firing on him!

Pete jumped up, waving his arms, yelling "Marines! Marines! Quit firing!"

A round zipped past his ear, but the firing stopped. Somebody over there had recognized they were friendlies. Of course, now that made him a target for the Chinese, but they seemed to be occupied with more immediately threatening Marines.

Pete flopped back down as Sgt McNamara somehow made it up to the building, back up against the wall. He took a grenade, pulled the pin, then stepped out a pace before lobbing it up to the roof. A second grenade followed before the first one detonated. Both explosions sounded muted, almost inconsequential, but the firing from the rooftop ceased.

Sgt McNamara looked back at Pete, then shrugged. He was committed now, and running back was probably more dangerous then staying where he was.

Chapter 22

Pagasa Island

When the explosions sounded, screams filled the rec center and people dove to lay flat. Not everyone dove down, though. As the Chinese soldiers spun around to look out, groups of men jumped up to take them on.

Analiza was trampled by one man as he joined the rush to get to the nearest soldier. Either through complacency or because he was focusing on the fighting that had broken out outside, the soldier didn't see the group that gang-tackled him.

A shot rang out inside the community center, then another. One of the soldiers was not so complacent, and he fired into the men rushing him. It didn't stop the wave of angry men, but two went down before the soldier disappeared beneath the mass.

Analiza jumped up. Three Chinese soldiers were down. But the planning had not been enough. One soldier had not been rushed, and now he faced the 200 + people in the center, weapon pointing at them. They could take him down, but at what cost?

Almost with a communal mind, the growing mass of people took a step closer to him. Analiza expected his weapon to open up, spewing death.

Suddenly, the soldier placed his weapon on the floor and said *"Ako ang iyong bilanggo"* in perfect, if accented, Tagolog. "I am your prisoner."

Several men rushed him, dragging him up against the wall. One man, Philip Ramos, grabbed the man's rifle, and thrust it under the soldier's chin.

"I'm going to blow your head off," he threatened.

"Stop that," Analiza shouted, bulling her way up and pushing the muzzle of the rifle down.

"He could have fired upon us. But he chose not to. We are not animals here."

"They took our island. They killed our soldiers. I'll fucking kill him if I want," Philip yelled back.

"That's not for you to decide," she yelled, the strength of her will forcing Philip to take a step back. "For all they've done, they have treated us as well as could be hoped for. They haven't abused us. No rape, no murder. We are Christian people. We are God-fearing. And this is how you want to act? This is how you want your children to see us?"

That seemed to back down the crowd. The fierce firing outside seemed to fade a bit as the adrenaline faded back a notch.

"OK, tie him up, along with the other two," Val Williams said.

Analiza looked around. Two other soldiers, looking worse for wear, were also being held by groups of men. She then spotted the fourth soldier. He had been the one who had gotten off two shots, and he had paid the price for that. His bloody body lay still on the floor.

Analiza backed down as Val began to organize. Their own soldiers were released, then the four Chinese rifles given to them. Without knowing just who was fighting outside, the decision was made for everyone to stay put. The Filipino soldiers would protect them but not leave to join the fighting going on outside in the town.

Chapter 23
Pagasa Island

Sgt Jay McNamara stood with his back alongside the building. He wasn't sure what had made him jump up and make the run. It had been instinct, not conscious thought. He trembled a bit at the thought. He wasn't sure how he had made it through the friendly fire to the relative safety of the building.

He had thrown the two grenades blindly, but at least one of them seemed to have taken effect. The sniper appeared to be out of commission.

He looked back at Lt Van Slyke, who was now flopped down in the open, and shrugged. He wasn't sure what he was supposed to do next. Running back would likely invite more fire. If he moved to the north side of the building, then First Platoon might mistake him for a Chinese soldier and take him under fire. Then there were the Chinese. He could hear them shouting inside. If they realized he was there, they could simply shoot through the walls and probably hit him.

The building he was up against was the one on the far west side of the community, which seemed logical as a building with noisy pumps and generators would be located further from the living areas. Most of First Platoon would be focused on the government building, but he had to assume that someone would be assigned to this one. It sucked not having comm. He should be able to contact the other units and coordinate something.

He got down low and began to creep forward. He wanted to peek around the front of the building and see what was happening. Just as he was passing beneath a window, a rifle came poking out. He froze, not moving a muscle. If the rifleman came forward just a bit and looked down, he would be spotted.

His team must have seen that as well as they opened up on the window, splinters of wood raining down on him. The rifleman opened up, spraying rounds back into the tree line. This soldier was not a coward, Jay had to admit.

He felt down into his pocket. Two more grenades left. Rolling over, he took one, pulled the pin, and motioned back to his team to cease fire. Once they did, he took a deep breath, then stood up, hand grabbing the rifle barrel, forcing it up as the soldier continued to fire a few rounds. With his left hand still grabbing the barrel, he threw the grenade into the room, just getting it past the startled face of the Chinese soldier. In one more motion, he reached down, grabbed his Colt, and fired two rounds into the base of the soldier's neck. The man dropped, and he could see motion as two or three other soldiers shouted and started to swing their own weapons toward him.

Rounds came through the window and the walls themselves as Jay dropped to the ground. As the grenade exploded, shrapnel also went through the wooden walls. If he had remained standing, his own grenade might have taken him out.

A chattering of an automatic weapon opened up, sounding like it was coming from the far side of the building. There was still at least someone left alive in there, someone firing at their fellow Marines. Whoever it was had to be stopped.

He glanced back towards his team, and he was surprised to see Cpl Holleran and LCpl Maus pelting towards him. They had moved forward while Jay was engaged, and by doing so, when they left the tree line to join him, the building itself had masked them from Third Platoon, keeping them out of sight. Jay realized that he should have done the same thing.

It only took a few moments until both dropped down beside him.

"The lieutenant sent us to join you," Holleran breathlessly told him. "We need to clear this building, then hold it until Kilo can link up with us."

Another burst of the automatic weapon inside was an exclamation mark on the need to clear the building.

"OK, wait a sec."

Jay popped up, glanced inside the window opening, then fell back immediately.

"I think there're three inside here, but they look to be down. Give me a boost, and I'm going in. Then you, Maus, you're smaller. You can cover me while I pull you in, Holleran.

"OK, push hard. I want to fly through the window," he told them.

The two Marines took him as his word, almost bodily lifting the big sergeant and throwing him inside the building. Jay hit the dead body of the soldier he had killed, then rolled on the floor, bringing his M4 to bear.

Another soldier lay facedown, motionless, blood pooling underneath him. The third soldier in the room was sitting, but he was obviously in bad shape. Part of his jaw was gone, and below his flak jacket, his thighs were bloody. His rifle was out of a few feet from him, and he was feebly trying to reach it. Jay started to pull his trigger, but something stopped him. He stood up and kicked the soldier's weapon away. The man let his hand fall, then looked up, resignation in his eyes.

Jay simply turned away, then reached out the window to help LCpl Maus in.

"Watch him," was all he told the younger Marine as he helped the bigger Cpl Holleran in through the window.

Cpl Holleran raised his eyebrows when he saw the still-living Chinese soldier.

Jay picked up all three Chinese weapons and tossed them out the window.

"If he makes it, he makes it. He's no threat to us now. Come on, we've got to put that machine gun out of commission."

The room they were in looked to be some sort of store room. Going right by the book, the three of them might as well have been training back at combat town, clearing the building step-by-step. They made their way quickly through the machine shop and the generator room. The machine gun sounded up ahead in what was probably the building's office.

There was a loud explosion that seemed to shut down the automatic weapon, but after a pause, it opened up again. Whatever their fellow Marines had just tried, it hadn't worked.

They got up to the door of the office. The Chinese soldiers were counting on their fellow soldiers to cover their rear, but they would still be on the alert for an attack from that direction. The three Marines needed to hit them hard and fast. Cpl Holleran sidled to the far side of the door. Jay was going in high, Maus low.

He held up one hand, then signaled a countdown: three...two...one.

On one, both he and Holleran moved forward, kicking in the door. All three Marines opened up, taking the two Chinese soldiers under their sights, likely before the soldiers' brains even registered what was happening. The two Chinese soldiers probably never realized that they were under fire before three bursts cut their lives short.

They stood there for a moment, staring at the two soldiers. Two men, who a moment ago, and been breathing, hearts beating. Now they were just meat.

"Well, fuck them, too." Holleran said.

Jay didn't quite know exactly what that meant, but he never-the-less wholeheartedly agreed with the corporal.

A few rounds came in through the window, sending them scrambling back out the door.

"Maus, go find a white sheet or something. We need to let the rest of the Marines know this building is secure."

It wasn't until he said it that it hit home. The building was secure. It was no longer in Chinese hands. It was now in the hands of the US Marine Corps.

Chapter 24
Beijing

"So where is the *Jinggan Shan now"* asked General Chen.

"This is the ship, General," the technician responded, pointing to an icon on the screen. "It should arrive off of Thitu in approximately two hours."

"And when will the repairs be made on the *Changbai Shan?*"

"Senior Captain Chou reports that it will be at least 24 more hours" interjected Commander Hung.

General Li tried to look calm, but inside, his anxiety was rising. General Chen had decided he wanted to see the command center and had brought along with him Major General Guo from the Fourth Department and Admiral Ding, the Chief of Staff of the PLA Navy. Li had no issue with Admiral Ding, but he knew that his actions with regards to cyber-warfare and communications would have rubbed the major general the wrong way, causing a loss of face. His little operation, after all, had made the Fourth Department look like fools, a price he had been willing to pay at the time, but that he now hoped wouldn't come back to bite him.

General Chen looked at the screen for a moment, then turned to Li and ordered, "I want the *Jinggan Shan* to hold in place for the moment while I absorb the entire situation. I don't like making a piecemeal assault, and I would rather have both ships able to assault in unison to keep the enemy from focusing their forces. I have already ordered General Li to begin preparing the air assets should I give the OK, but before I do that, I must ensure that your plan will not only work, but work with a minimal loss of life."

General Li inwardly groaned, but he let none of that show. The stupid chief of staff was going to waste the opportunity with his cautious approach. He thought to Sun Tzu's dictum:

Those who arrive early at the place of conflict will be in a position to take initiative.

Those who arrive late must hasten into action troubled.

Thus, those are skilled in conflicts will make the first move to prevent others from taking initiative.

General Chen was going to let the Americans become entrenched, and that could essentially end the operation before it really got started. He wished he knew what the situation was on Thitu, but he hadn't the opportunity to ask Sung Wenyan for an update, something he wanted to receive in private.

"So with the *Jinggan Shan* holding for the time being and the *Changbai Shan* making repairs, we have a moment to use all our assets to bring about a positive solution. Major General Guo, I want you to leave some of your best soldiers here at this command center to ensure we do not waste our superior cyber-warfare capabilities. Admiral Ding, please have someone assist Commander Hung here in the command center. He is doing a fine job, of course, but the better staffed we are, the better our chances at success."

General Li noticed the deft handling of that. General Chen obviously wanted his own men present in the command center, but he also knew who Hung's father was, and if things didn't go well, he didn't want to be at odds with any of the high-ranking PLA generals and admirals if it came to finger-pointing time. Chen might be too cautious now, but the man was the penultimate politician.

As General Chen looked back at the screen, Li sidled aside, motioning with a quick nod of his head for Sung Wenyan to join him.

Without looking directly at him, he asked in a low voice, "Mr. Sung, what is the situation on Thitu now?"

Sung glanced at his boss before looking straight ahead and responded, "Communications remain spotty, but the island has fallen to the Americans."

"Fallen? Completely?" he whispered, surprise making it hard to keep his voice down.

"Yes, General. Our forces have been neutralized."

General Li was shocked. Major Ching was one of the best young field officers in the entire PLA. Even if he was outnumbered, he could have kept the fight going for days in the dense jungle on the island. It was inconceivable that the man would surrender or be defeated in such a short amount of time. This made the situation even more desperate. The entire operation was slipping away. They could not afford to waste any more time.

"Mr. Sung. Order Senior Captain Chou to commence the assault on Thitu. The island will be taken, and taken now."

Sung Wenyan said nothing. Li could feel the anger begin to build. He knew exactly what Sung was doing. He was weighing his options, wondering with whom he should hitch his wagon. And even if he decided to go along with his orders, Sung wanted him to realize that he had options.

"And General Chen's orders?" Sung asked, his voice a whisper.

"With our current communications problems, General Chen's most recent orders could not be received, I believe, when we most assuredly tried to relay them."

"But we have no communications problems with the ships, only with Major Ching's forces, general."

"You are a bright man, Sung Wenyan. You have capabilities, for which you have been rewarded. I am sure you will find a reasonable solution for this issue."

"Yes, I have been rewarded, to an extent, that is..."

Li felt filthy bargaining like this. Duty and patriotism brooked no question, no grasping for personal rewards. But he would do what he had to do to ensure the mission's success.

"Yes, and many more will come to you, Sung Wenyan. Remember, I answer to higher authority on this, and they have much more leeway in expressing their gratitude for services rendered."

They stood there, side-by-side, neither looking at the other while General Chen spoke with Major General Chou and a young captain, gesturing at the status of forces screen.

Finally, he heard the words he wanted to hear.

"I believe that the communications problems have spread to our capital ships, general. I will ensure that they receive the correct and most worthy orders."

General Li did not let the relief he felt show in his face or posture. He wished he could have those air assets now, but it would be better to launch immediately before the Americans could get more assets to the island. This operation had to be completed, and completed now. Taiping may be out of the question at the moment, but Thitu could be back in Chinese hands by the end of the day.

Chapter 25
Pagasa Island

Sergeant Harrington Steptoe sat to the side, along with Lt Van Slyke and 1stLt Landon Gaines, the Third Platoon commander, while the skipper, the XO, and the first sergeant spoke with the Chinese captain. One of the Marines from Second Platoon spoke Chinese, but only to an extent, so it was a relief to discover that the captain spoke excellent English.

His arm had been bandaged, and he didn't seem too reluctant to talk. He seemed more surprised than anything that the Americans had gotten involved. From his point of view, the Filipinos had instigated the conflict by arresting and holding Chinese fishermen, and their orders had been to finally take back territory that had been Chinese for hundreds of years.

Captain Dan something-or-other had been the second-in-command, but on the first pass of the Osprey, their commanding officer had taken a round that had shattered his helmet and killed him.

Capt Niimoto had remarked that he was surprised that the Chinese had chosen to defend the buildings, something that fixed them in place. So Steptoe wondered if that lucky volley from the Osprey had changed the course of the fight. Perhaps a more seasoned commander would have retreated into the dense vegetation that covered the northern 2/3's of the island.

Gunny Dailey came up and interrupted, telling the skipper that the water and electricity had been turned back on. The Chinese captain's eyes widened at that. Steptoe knew that the Filipinos had turned off both, telling the Chinese that the generator had been taken out in the initial Chinese assault.

A wry smile came over the captain's face as he took that in. It had to be a tough position for him. He had lost over half of his men in the fight, and the rest had been taken prisoner.

The Marines had not gotten away unscathed, either. LCpl Kenny had only been the first to fall. Seven other Marines had been KIA with another 15 and one Navy corpsman wounded in the assault. With the other recon Marine who had been hit by friendly fire, that was 25 Marine and Navy casualties, more casualties in one single assault than in any attack back in Afghanistan and Iraq, maybe more than anything going back to Vietnam or even Korea.

When the count had reached the skipper, it looked like someone had punched him in the gut. But to Steptoe, he was surprised the number had been so that low. When the Chinese had opened up with their automatic weapons, Steptoe had been sure that First Platoon would be mowed down as they rushed from the tree line into the built-up area. If it hadn't been for the initial supporting fire coming from the Second Platoon from the south and fixing the Chinese attention in that direction, and then for the intense supporting fire throughout the assault, he was sure the casualties would have been even higher.

He knew Tony, as he still privately thought of him, would be second-guessing himself, but the Chinese, despite fighting from the relative protection of the buildings, had taken even more casualties. And these were professional, competent soldiers, not jumped-up farmers with rifles.

The Chinese captain was friendly, even talkative, but he wasn't offering much of value. He didn't seem too taken aback by his surrender, although he wasn't too happy that three of his seriously wounded soldiers had been medivac'd back to the *Makin Island* along with 1stLt Ayers, Cpl Finnegan, and PFC Stuckey, all seriously wounded in the assault. He kept asking when his soldiers would be returned to him. When it seemed as if he had nothing more to say other than ask to see to his men, the skipper had him escorted back inside the community center where his surviving soldiers were being kept and having their wounds treated.

"I think he's pretty complacent for someone who just had his butt kicked," First Sergeant Davidson growled as the Chinese captain left.

"You're right," added the skipper. "I have the feeling that the Chinese have got something else up their sleeves. I don't want to lose the Osprey we have here now for a recon, but as soon as the medivac bird or the other one returns and we have two on deck, I want one to do a thorough recon of the northern part of this island as well as the little islands surrounding us. I don't know what the CO has for us now, and I won't know until an Osprey gets back with our orders, but I want Second and Third to stay on full alert. First," he directed at SSgt Willis, the new acting platoon commander, "keep assisting the Filipino civilians, but don't let them wander off. They're not our prisoners, but I don't want a gaggle here until we've a better grasp of the situation."

"Aye-aye, sir," the bulky staff sergeant responded with a firm voice.

SSgt Willis was a gym rat, a Harlem boy who had taken to the Marines like the proverbial duck to water. Steptoe had caught a few glimpses of him rallying his Marines when Lt Ayers had gone down, fearless in the heavy Chinese fire as he got his Marines into the buildings almost by his force of will alone.

"Lt Van Slyke, I'd like you to take the higher buildings, maybe the government building there and the control tower and just keep an eye on things. Until our comm is back, it'll be your Mark-one eyeballs that'll be our early warning.

"Other than that, we've already got our orders. Let's get everyone fed and watered. When the Osprey gets back, we'll know what battalion wants us to do, so until then, just keep on the alert."

There was a chorus of 'aye-aye's' as the platoon commanders and the XO moved off.

"That means you there, lieutenant," Steptoe couldn't resist telling Lt Van Slyke before he was able to head off.

"Huh?"

"The skipper said 'watered.' That means you. You stink like, well, like piss. You need to get hosed down!"

Van Slyke tried to glare as Steptoe burst into laughter, but he couldn't keep it up and broke out into a laugh himself.

"So you heard about that?" he asked.

"Lieutenant, everybody's heard about it."

"Oh, just fucking great! That's all I need now," he muttered as he strode away.

Sgt Steptoe merely laughed again.

Chapter 26
Pagasa Island

1st Lt Peter Van Slyke gave a quiet chuckle as he turned on the faucet. He had given Gunny Sloan the orders before excusing himself to find a hose. Stepchild giving him grief was a bit hard to take, especially when it was warranted. He'd have to get back at him later, but at least two-fold.

It had taken the Filipino engineer literally only minutes to get the island's generator going again, and with power, the pumps were working as well. But with the water flowing, the Filipino civilians had eagerly crowded all the available showers and faucets, forcing the pumps to labor to provide enough pressure for all the demanding thirsty and ripe-smelling people.

With his Marines being positioned, enough time had elapsed that Pete had access to a faucet alone. He pulled off his helmet and body armor before turning the water over his head. He had actually gotten used to the smell of the urine, but once the water hit him, it was almost as if it was reconstituting it, bringing forth that harsh, ammonia smell.

He pulled off his utilities top, letting the water splash against his body, letting it carry away not only the piss, but the grime, the sweat, the ants—everything that had taken a place on his skin. He closed his eyes and luxuriated in the feeling.

"Excuse me," a soft voice broke through his reverie.

He glanced in back of him to see a slender Filipina with huge doe eyes staring at him. Half naked, there was nothing to hide the scars that had ravaged his face. With his fellow Marines, he had gotten to the point that he rarely thought of the scars. But with women he became much more self-conscious.

He reflexively jerked the hose he was holding, sending some water towards the girl, making her dance a step to the right to avoid getting wet.

"Oh, sorry! I didn't mean that," he stammered out.

"Oh, don't worry! You didn't get me, but after the last few days, it wouldn't matter. I don't think I'll ever complain about getting wet again."

"Oh...yea, I guess so. I mean, I know what you mean....I guess."

They stood there looking at each other, water still flowing from the hose, making an arc as it fell to the ground.

"So, um, can I help you?" he asked, trying to maneuver a bit so that the scarred side of his face was away from her.

"Are you Lieutenant Slyke?" she asked.

"Um, Lieutenant Van Slyke, yes."

"Oh, I'm sorry. I thought he said 'Lieutenant Slyke.' But it is 'Van Slyke.'"

"And you're looking for me?" he asked her.

"Oh, yes. This is so embarrassing. I just came to apologize, but now I'm embarrassed to say so."

Then it dawned on Pete. With her hair newly washed and brushed back, with clean clothes, and in the daylight, she looked different, but this was the same girl who had thrown the bucket of piss on him, the one who had then come back out and warned him.

"Ah," he exclaimed, "That was you!"

"Yes, it was," she said, obviously knowing that he now recognized her, "and I am so sorry!"

"Sorry? For what?"

She looked at him in surprise, as if trying to see if he was serious.

"For throwing the pee on you. If I had seen you, I would never have done it!"

Pete couldn't help it, and he broke out into a laugh. She looked at him like he was crazy.

"That's nothing, um, miss. I was so amazed when you came back out, when you gave me the information on the enemy. That was brave."

"But, but, I still, I mean … it's an insult to do that, right?"

"Don't worry about it, Miss…?" he prompted.

"Oh, sorry. I don't know my manners. I'm Analiza Reyes. Pleased to meet you, Lieutenant Van Slyke."

She held out her hand, which Pete took and solemnly shook. She spoke excellent English, but Pete liked the way her accent handled his name.

"You can call me Pete. Can I call you Analiza?"

Pete could swear she blushed as she looked down.

"Of course, uh, Pete."

"Analiza, what you did was very brave, to risk yourself like that."

She said nothing, and he realized he was still holding her hand. He dropped it. Suddenly, he felt awkward.

"Well, I'm glad we were able to meet in better conditions," he said as he couldn't come up with anything more astute or clever. "But I need to finish cleaning, then get back to my men."

"Oh, of course. Sorry to disturb you. I will leave you now," she said hurriedly.

"Oh, you didn't disturb me. I'm glad to meet you, and I hope we have a chance to speak again."

"Of course. If you want. Well, I'll let you finish your bath."

She immediately turned and strode off. Pete just stood there and watched her leave. She was petite, but he appreciated her figure as she walked. It was only as she went around the corner of the building and was out of sight that he realized that for a few moments, he had forgotten his scars and had actually spoken to her as guys normally spoke to girls.

It was a nice feeling while it lasted, but then the awkwardness kicked in, and he knew it would never go anywhere anyway. He would be off the island soon, on to his next mission. And while she hadn't seemed to focus on his face, he knew that was merely because she had been embarrassed about the bucket of piss. In another setting, she would be rather turned off by his appearance.

It didn't really bother him that much. He was used to it. He pulled the hose back and let the water hit his face. It was going to be good to feel clean again.

Chapter 27
Pagasa Island

"And that's basically it," Major Cannon told the skipper. "You're to hold your position here while the diplomats do what diplomats do. The word we're getting from DoD is that by holding Thitu and Taiping, we're giving our side a big advantage while they hit the Chinese at the UN and at the various embassies. It's all above my pay grade. Yours too. We don't want war, but we have to think that the Chinese don't either."

"With all due respect sir, I've got nine Marines dead. I kinda call that war," Capt Niimoto replied, bitterness evident in his voice.

Sgt Steptoe knew the feeling. LCpl Kenny's death had hit him pretty hard, too, more so now that he had a couple of hours to dwell on it.

"No one's going to deny that, captain. But in the big picture, war with China is something neither of us can afford. The world can't afford it.

"So now, just hold fast. You're going to have one plane here on station at all times. We'll have one on Taiping, too, and the other two will be working as couriers. When the *Makin Island* gets a little closer, we'll be augmented with the helos, but until then, it's our four Ospreys."

"What about Likas Island?" the skipper asked.

"OK, I'm a little confused again. Likas Island is which one?" the major asked.

"We call it West York Island, but the Filipinos call it Likas. Just like Thitu is called Pagasa Island by the Filipinos. The Filipinos had a small detachment on Likas-slash-West-York that the Chinese here told them they took."

"I think we've done what we were supposed to do, and the two big prizes here are in American hands. I'll pass this back to the

MEU, and I'm sure they'll pass it up, but I doubt we'll take any action on it. Let the Chinese hold it for now. We've put the diplomats in a position of power, so hopefully, all of this'll be over soon. We'll scold the Chinese, slap their wrists, then it'll be business as usual."

"Don't you think that sucks, sir?" Lt Hosseini, the XO asked.

"Ours is not to reason why, there, lieutenant. But think of it this way. The Chinese are the biggest holder of American debt. The Americans are the biggest buyers of Chinese products. If we went to all-out war, think of the effects on not only our two economies, but the world's economy. I'm not saying it doesn't suck. I'm just being practical. If there's any way to avoid war, then we're going to avoid it. Kilo Company has done your duty, at a heavy price, to make sure we not only avoid war, but we do it in a way to our best advantage."

The company headquarters was silent as they all digested this. Steptoe knew the major was right, but that didn't make it any more palatable.

"What about the prisoners?" Capt Niimoto asked the major.

"Well, as to that, I don't know. I left you the Navy intel team," he said, referring to the three sailors and one Marine who were now busy interviewing the prisoners, "but other than that, I guess it's the status quo. Just keep them under wraps for now. I'll pass your concerns to the MEU CO when I get back.

"OK, if there's nothing else, I need to take off. You've got Captain Nance here for the moment. You got anything else for me?"

"Doc Ski wants two more Marines medivac'd, if you could. But no, other than that, that's about it," the skipper told him.

"No problem," was the reply. "Get them loaded up, and as soon as they're aboard, I'm outa here."

They watched the major walk back to his Osprey. Steptoe knew he was only the messenger, but he still felt a degree of anger towards what he had said. Somehow, it seemed to diminish what they had sacrificed.

"OK, gunny, let's get the ammo and chow distributed," the skipper ordered, pointing to the supply drop the major had brought with his flight. "And let the mayor or whatever you call him know I would like to see him."

Steptoe looked around as people bustled about, all with jobs to do. As the company comm chief, he felt a bit out of place. Comm was still out, and after re-laying the wire, there wasn't much for him to do.

As he thought about it, though, maybe that was a good thing. If he had nothing to do until the ambassadors and all the higher-ups could get all of this straightened out, all the better.

Chapter 28
Pagasa Island

"Come on, eat up, Joselito," Analiza said, holding another spoon of soup for the small boy to take in his mouth.

He seemed to be interested in just about everything else other than eating. The big American plane getting ready to take off seemed to be particularly interesting to him.

From the terror of the fighting only a couple of hours ago, things had calmed down quickly. The Americans had asked that they stick together, so communal dining had become the choice for a late lunch. It was almost a festival atmosphere despite the presence of the 25 or so Chinese prisoners being kept in one corner of the community center and guarded by four Americans and six of their recently freed Filipino soldiers. Another handful of Americans kept coming over and taking one of the Chinese soldiers over to the front office before returning him and getting another.

"Analiza, there's your boyfriend," Satin remarked, eliciting a fit of giggle from the others.

"He's not my boyfriend," she protested before looking up to catch sight of the young lieutenant walking up to the city offices.

"How did you know who I was talking about, then?" Satin asked laughingly.

"I don't have a boyfriend, thank you very much, so whoever you meant couldn't have been mine," she replied.

She watched Lt Van Slyke, no, Pete, as he walked. He had an assured gait, full of confidence. Even from this distance, she could see the scar which marred his face. It had taken her aback a bit when she had first seen it, but she thought it gave him character and hinted at experiences perhaps better left unmentioned. Her imagination couldn't help but wonder how he had gotten the scars, though.

"Methinks she doth protest too much," quoted Honey, causing her own share of giggles.

"You know," Satin went on, "I don't know how you do it in Cebu, but in parts of the Philippines, throwing pee on a man is a proposal of marriage."

"Oh, that's not true," Analiza exclaimed as the others broke out into peals of laughter.

"How do you know? I think they do that in the north of Luzon. I mean, they smoke their dead ancestors and leave them in caves. So who's to say they don't use pee as a marriage proposal?"

By now, everyone was laughing, even the youngsters who might not quite have understood what the laughing was about but simply got caught up in the overall merriment.

"Satin, you know that's not true," she said even if she was smiling as she said it.

It was good to laugh. They had been under so much pressure, and friends had lost their lives. Now, with the arrival of the Americans, they felt the worst was over, and the simple act of laughter was really the best medicine.

She realized that Satin and the others were teasing, and she didn't mind. They were all friends. But she couldn't help but to wonder as she watched Pete enter the building and disappear from view just what he was really like. She'd only had a few words with him, really, but still, ...

Chapter 29
Pagasa Island

Sgt Jay McNamara leaned back on one of the two rickety chairs, sipping at the warm coke. The remains of some fried chicken and rice were on the paper plate he put on the built-in wooden work station that fronted the windows of the control tower.

Cpl Holleran was in the other chair while the rest of the team was sitting on the floor, eating the chow the Filipinos had given them. Rank had its privileges, and as the two senior Marines, he and Holleran had proper chairs.

Of course, "proper" was all subjective, just as calling this a control tower was perhaps a little generous. Oh, it had a radio for communications with incoming flights, and it was the tallest structure on the island and so had views down to the runway, but without any sort of radar or other more modern equipment, it seemed like some kid's treehouse, more than anything else. Even the rusted, flimsy ladder they had to climb up to get into the structure at the top seemed less-than-permanent.

At least the windows that gave the tower a 360 view were in good shape and nominally clean. Jay took another sip from the coke as he glanced around the waters surrounding the island. As soon as the others finished eating, they would take over the watch.

In back of him, away from the runway, the heavy jungle that covered the northern 2/3's of the island looked inviting, like some sort of resort. That was a far cry from reality, though. The dense brush was almost impenetrable, and Jay still had gouges where the branches had stabbed him as he had made his way through it.

LCpl Maus burped, then got up and went out the back door to the metal grill platform that connected to the ladder. He stood at the low rail, then casually started to unbutton his trousers.

"What the fuck do you think you're doing, Maus?" Jay called out.

The lance corporal spun around, confusion on his face.

"I'm taking a piss, sergeant," he told him, stating the obvious.

"Not here you're not. Those are civilians down there, and they don't need to look up and see your dick flapping in the breeze. Besides, you'd probably splatter all over the ladder, and I ain't going to be putting my hand on that when I climb down. Get your ass down the ladder and go use one of the heads."

Maus had the grace to look sheepish as he buttoned back up. He went to the ladder and started making his way down. Cpl Holleran caught Jay's eyes and shrugged his shoulders. Mighty Maus was actually a gung ho Marine, but sometimes, he just didn't think.

"Police up your trash," Holleran told the others, handing out a plastic bag.

LCpl Brugal dumped his trash in the bag, then stepped out to the railing, stretching. He stood there, taking a smoke break. Jay wasn't a smoker and didn't understand why someone would smoke right after eating, but better on the railing than inside the tower proper.

Jay looked back down to the runway. There was a fishing boat tied up at the pier on the far eastern side of the runway, the same boat the Chinese had used to first get on the island. A few smaller boats were there as well. In the middle of the runway, right where the open area and the lone road had been cut to lead from it to the town, the Osprey sat like some sort of huge insect. The back ramp was down, and Jay could see the figures of two Marines lying back on it, out of the sun.

"Hey, what kind of ship is that?" Brugal asked to no one in particular.

Jay turned around, looking to the waters surrounding the north side of the island. He didn't see anything, so he got up and stepped outside.

"Where?" he asked.

"Look, over there," LCpl Brugal responded, pointing to the west.

Jay refocused his line of sight, and there, in the distance, he could make out the large grey shape of a ship. It wasn't a merchant ship, that was for sure.

"Is that the *Makin Island*?" asked Cpl Destafney, stepping beside the two of them.

It was hard to see, but it kind of had the same general shape. But it couldn't be.

"No, the *Makin Island* won't be here until sometime tomorrow, and I don't think the Filipinos have anything like that," Jay responded.

It seemed to register with all of them at the same time.

"Shit, I bet it's Chinese," DeStafney said for all of them.

Jay stepped back into the tower, then grabbed the landline they had installed, picking up the phone Sgt Steptoe had given them. He keyed the handset twice, then listened. He keyed it again. Nothing.

Stepping back out, he turned towards the rest of the buildings and screamed out, "Steptoe, get on the hook now!"

Chapter 30
Pagasa Island

Sgt Steptoe was leaning back, almost drowsing. The fried chicken the Filipinos had given them hit the spot, and the lack of sleep lately was catching up to him. The skipper and the first sergeant were conferring, so it didn't seem like his services were in high demand at the moment.

"Steptoe, that recon sergeant's yelling for you," Sgt Issac's voice woke him up.

"What?" he asked stupidly.

"Up there, in the control tower. That recon team leader. He's yelling for you to get on the phone."

Steptoe shook his head, and only then faintly heard the buzzing of someone wanting to be heard on the phone. He got up and went to the table where he had set up his phone handset.

"Yea, this is headquarters, over"

"It's about time. I think we've got company. There's a big ship coming, and I think it's Chinese, over"

"Are you sure?" Steptoe asked, forgetting the "over."

"No, I'm not sure. I don't have Wiki imbedded in my brain. But it ain't American, and I don't think it's Filipino. That leaves Chinese, over."

"OK, let me get the skipper. Wait one, over."

He put down the handset and rushed out the door. Capt Niimoto was with 1stSgt Davidson, deep in discussion. Steptoe ran up to them.

"Skipper, I think you need to talk to McNamara. He says there's a Chinese ship coming."

Sgt Steptoe expected the captain to come back to the phone. Instead, he took off for the control tower, the first sergeant with him. Steptoe had to agree that made more sense, so he took off in trace.

The skipper was already halfway up the ladder by the time Sgt Steptoe got to the base of the tower. He climbed up, wishing he had some gloves. The rust bit into his hands as he climbed.

The railing alongside the back of the control tower was crowded by the time Steptoe made it up. The skipper was looking through a pair of binos off to the west.

He slowly brought the binos down before saying, "Yea, it's Chinese. I can make out the flag. We have to assume it's not coming to apologize. First Sergeant Davidson, let's get all the actuals together right now. I would guess we've got 40 minutes, maybe more until it gets here. I want to make sure we all understand our missions."

He spun around, pushing past Steptoe to head on back down the ladder. Steptoe turned to follow him as the 1stSgt clapped McNamara on the shoulder.

"Good job, Jesus. Keep an eye on him and let us know what he's up to," he told him.

Sgt Steptoe knew that the 1stSgt and McNamara went back to their time on the *Dunham*, but it still sounded weird to hear McNamara called "Jesus." He was "Jay" to pretty much everyone else. Jay or Sgt McNamara.

Steptoe got to the ground and ran after the skipper, who was shouting for all the principles.

"I want the mayor, too," he added, trusting someone to get the man.

Steptoe was puffing by the time he reached the city offices. The building had been pretty shot up, but it was still solid and offered some degree of shelter.

The skipper was already giving orders, or more specifically, reiterating what he had previously ordered. He was not going to get caught in the same trap as the Chinese had. The buildings in the town had no strategic value. There was no reason to stay in them, becoming known targets. He was going to use the jungle to defend the island, to make it difficult for anyone to pry them out.

They weren't going to give up a toehold, either, like the Japanese did on so many islands during WWII. Second Platoon would occupy the tree line on the east half of the runway, Third Platoon the west side. First Platoon and Weapons would occupy the tree line to the south of the town, providing cover and support as the two platoons pulled back or to reinforce either of the other two platoons in the offense. No one mentioned that this was an awfully large frontage for the company.

"Mr. Mayor," he said, as that worthy came up. "It looks like the Chinese are not done with us. An amphibious ship is bearing down on us, and they could have between 1,000 and maybe up to 2,000 soldiers on board. I want you to evacuate as many of the women and children as possible on that fishing boat. That boat can easily make it to the mainland. I want your Filipino soldiers to escort them, " he said, nodding to the Filipino lieutenant who had just arrived. "and for those who can't fit in the boat, they need to get into the jungle, as far north as possible."

"That's not going to happen, captain," the Filipino lieutenant told him.

"What do you mean?"

"We've got twelve of us who are ready to fight. This is our land, and we're not leaving."

Capt Niimoto looked at the defiant lieutenant. Sgt Steptoe knew he was weighing his options. The skipper knew what his Marines could do, how they would fight together. These Filipinos were an unknown factor, and if they could free up Marines by escorting the civilians, then all the better.

"I think that you would serve best by protecting your fellow citizens, and as the commanding officer here, I think ..." the skipper started before being interrupted.

"With all due respect, sir, you hold no authority over me. This is the Philippines, and you are here as our guests. Welcome guests, but still guests. Technically, I'm in charge here, not you, not Mayor Lopez. So no matter what you're saying, we're staying. We can fight together or separately, I don't care. But fight we will."

Steptoe knew the skipper was a pragmatic man. So he was not surprised that he accepted the lieutenant's ultimatum.

"Fine, we're happy to have you with us. If you can augment Second Platoon in the initial defense, I would appreciate it."

The lieutenant nodded, then saluted. Marines don't normally salute indoors, but Capt Niimoto returned the salute.

"Pete, in that case, I want you to escort the civilians down to that boat and get them underway. But this has to be done now. There isn't a reason to think that the Chinese will fire upon a fishing boat, but we don't know what're their orders. The island should mask the boat from the Chinese, but for how long, I don't know. So get it done now," he told Lt Van Slyke.

The recon lieutenant nodded, then hurried out the door and in the direction of the community center.

"We're pretty sure the ship can't approach from the west, right?" he directed the question to the mayor.

"Yes sir, that is right. We still have wreckage there of one of our Navy ships. If it's a big ship, that leaves only the south and the southeast corner."

"Then again, sir, just because the ship can't approach doesn't mean its landing craft and air can't hit us from anywhere," the first sergeant put in.

"Landing craft, and any kind of boat, would have to come in from the runway areas," the mayor responded. The reefs and jungle would be almost impossible for anything to land anywhere else."

"OK, good point, but the first sergeant's got a good point, too. We cannot assume anything. We're oriented to the south now, but we need to be flexible and to keep our eyes open.

"Captain Nance, I don't want your Osprey a sitting duck. Can you get up and around, off the runway?"

"No problem. I don't want to be a sitting duck, either. I think we can fit right in the boat basin. It'll be tight, but I've already had a look there" the pilot answered. "Between the trees and the drop into the basin, that should keep us out of sight until we take off."

"Look, I don't know how much time we have. And I don't know how many Chinese are coming. But we know our mission, and we've been trained well. Let's show them what the Marines can do!" the captain extolled them.

A chorus of "oorah's" greeted him. They were all ready for whatever was coming.

Chapter 31
Pagasa Island

Pete Van Slyke had already passed the word to the Filipinos, and he was surprised at how quickly the people had dropped what they were doing and were getting organized. One man had run off to get one of the island's trucks, another had volunteered to pilot the boat and had taken off on a small motorcycle to get it started up, and the rest were prioritizing just who would be leaving. It was women and children first, of course, but still, people were being quickly given numbers.

Pete had told them they had ten minutes, something he hadn't dreamed could happen, but as the old truck pulled up, children were already being loaded into the bed. Capt Niimoto came in along with the mayor to check on the progress.

"Sir, what about them?" the XO asked, tilting his head to indicate the prisoners.

Pete had actually forgotten about them, despite the fact that they were sitting in plain sight in the back of the community center. Some of them looked nervous, aware by the bustle of activity that something was up. Their captain didn't look nervous, but concerned might fit.

Captain Niimoto walked over to the seated prisoners and thought for a bit.

"Leave them here. Keep them restrained, but just leave them."

"Sir?" the XO asked. "But they know about us," the XO persisted.

"If it gets to that, then I think the folks on that ship are already going to know what they need to know," the skipper replied, mind made up.

"Captain, if I may," the Chinese captain asked from his sitting position. "I appreciate your treatment, but I would hate for there to be an accident, shall we say. I am sure you have taken our national flag as a trophy, but perhaps you could see to raise it over this building? I don't want our own forces to cause unnecessary casualties."

Pete thought that the Chinese captain had a lot of gall to ask that. His own side was about to attack, to try and kill Marines, and he wanted this favor?

"Captain, as one Asian to another, I ask this of you."

Capt Niimoto actually took a step forward.

"If we want to bring in race, your people tried to invade my ancestor's home more than once, only to be turned back by divine intervention," he said with some force. "And now, I am a fourth-generation US citizen, born and raised. So don't presume to think my racial background gives you and me any degree of kinship."

The Chinese captain blanched, obviously knowing he had overstepped.

"However, as an American Marine, it is my duty to protect my prisoners. When we prevail, I can come back and retrieve the flag. If by chance we don't prevail, well, I guess it won't matter much then, will it?"

The captain looked relieved, and he nodded his understanding.

"Thank you, sir, ..." he started, but Capt Niimoto had already turned away.

"Gunny, get the flag out and put in on top of the building. Do it quick, though, then get out of here."

He turned to Pete.

"You've got to get going. I don't know how much time we have, but it can't be much. Get these civilians out of here."

"Aye-aye, sir," he replied as he rushed outside.

The truck was packed, and Gunny Sloan had commandeered a pick-up. Pete jumped in and told the gunny to take off, motioning the bigger truck to follow. They had to keep the speed down. The truck behind them was overloaded, and an accident would be catastrophic.

Still, it only took a minute or so before they reached the runway, then it was straight shot down to the boat basin.

He looked to the west as they drove. The Chinese ship was much closer, but still quite a ways out. Pete could just make out the red Chinese ensign, though, with his naked eyes.

They pulled up to the pier, jumping out to help the civilians get off the truck. The children were essentially manhandled onboard. Some of the children were laughing at the new game, but others started to cry. Women tried to hush them.

The boat didn't look that big, but all the children managed to get on board and almost all of the women as well. One middle-aged woman refused to leave her husband, insisting that they stay together. Pete didn't argue.

The Filipino on the helm called out, saying that they shouldn't take any more, that they would be dangerously overloaded. Pete called to stop the loading and told the man at the helm to pull out.

He was surprised then when one person jumped off the boat and back onto the pier. That surprise turned to concern when he realized it was Analiza. He rushed up to her.

"Why'd you get off?" he asked.

She looked flushed, but her reply was calm and collected. "I only wanted to help the kids get settled. And there're others who really needed to be on that boat, mothers of the kids, you know."

The boat was already pulling away, so nothing could be done about that. Some of the men, though, were going down to the small fishing boats that were tied up in the basin. They were going to head out, not to the mainland, but to some of the neighboring islets until it would be safe for them to come back.

"OK, but go with one of them, then," he implored.

"Sorry, Pete, but I don't like small *bangkas*. They make me sick. So I'm staying here," she firmly told him.

One of the aircrew came riding up on a very small, beat-up motorcycle.

"Get these boats out of here, now!" he shouted.

Coming down the runway, hugging the trees, but not airborne, the Osprey was making its way to the basin. There was a flurry of activity as the small fishing boats cast off and got underway.

Pete looked around. There were about 15 Filipinos left, and he knew there were another 30 or so still back in the town. He was supposed to take them into the jungle and out of harm's way.

"Gunny, let's get these people back. Load them back up."

As gunny shouted out orders, he took Analiza by the arm, pulling and pushing her up into the pickup's cab. He jumped in as it took off, pulling the door shut as gunny swung the truck around. They rocketed down the runway, the Chinese ship looking huge as it moved closer, but still a couple of miles out.

They turned and took the road into the town, which was already almost deserted. Of the Marines, only Gunny Dailey was in sight, along with a small Filipino working party, filling up some plastic bottles with water. A few other Filipinos were taking the filled bottles, then milling around.

As the trucks stopped and Pete jumped out, the gunny called out, "Sir, the skipper wants you out of here ASAP. Have everyone take some water, then you're supposed to go."

Gunny Sloan didn't wait for orders, but started directing their passengers to get the water. It took only a few minutes before everyone had at least one bottle of water and were looking at Pete for directions. Some had small backpacks on, others carried plastic shopping bags stuffed with what Pete hoped was food and not personal belongings. One older man had a roller bag. How he expected to take that into the jungle, well, Pete didn't have a clue.

He looked back over his shoulder. The Chinese ship was just clearing the tree line and coming into view. It was still a long ways out, but Pete knew they had to hurry.

"OK folks," he called out.

A few people looked to him, but others still milled about.

"Can I have your attention, please?" he called out again.

"Listen up!" bellowed Gunny Dailey.

All eyes, turned towards him, voices stilled.

"Thank you, gunny. OK, we don't really know what's going to happen, or if there's any danger. But better safe than sorry, so Captain Niimoto and Mayor Lopez have decided that we all need to fade into the jungle. I guess you've already got someone to lead the way?" he asked.

A middle-aged man stepped forward, touching his forefinger to the brim of the floppy hat he wore.

"In that case, lead on. Let's keep it tight, no straggling," he told them.

The guide and two others lead the group off. Cpl Schmidt and LCpl Viejes followed, weapons at the ready. As Pete fell in behind them, Analiza rushed up to join him. She gave a tentative smile as Pete looked back. He simply nodded. It wouldn't be any less dangerous up there with him than anywhere else. Pete hoped it wouldn't be dangerous at all, in fact.

The guide led them into the trees, entering the jungle on a small, barely noticed path. Pete took a glance behind him before he was swallowed up by the foliage. He had seven Marines and about 45 Filipinos with him. He hoped this was merely a precaution, that it was unnecessary.

They had gone into the jungle by about 100 meters when a soft, but distinct report sounded off in the distance. Only moments later, an explosion sounded behind them, coming from right about where the town would be.

Everyone stopped and turned around to look even if they were unable to see anything through the trees. The second battle for Pagasa Island had begun.

Chapter 32
Pagasa Island

Sgt Jay McNamara had watched his platoon commander and SSgt Tolbert's team lead the Filipinos into the woods. That left only his team and the mortar section still in the town. It was like the rest of the people, Marines and Filipinos alike, had simply disappeared.

The fishing boat evacuating some of the Filipinos had been visible, only a short way off the east side of the island and steaming north, and he could make out a scattering of small fishing boats fleeing. He knew the reasoning behind that, but it still had made him feel a bit abandoned.

When the ship had fired, it was almost anti-climatic. This was not the huge broadsides from battleships he had seen on The History Channel. There had been a flash, then a sharp retort. Moments later, he had actually heard the incoming round whistle through the air before it impacted on the city government building.

The explosion, while significant, was also less than he had expected. A hole had been blown out of one section of the second-story wall, but the building remained pretty much intact.

"That all they got?" LCpl Brugal asked.

"That's about it as far as guns. The biggest thing they have is a 3 incher," Cpl Holleran answered matter-of-factly.

Jay stopped to stare at his corporal.

How had he known that? he wondered.

If comm had been up, a quick search would have given him the same information, but somehow Holleran had that information at his beck and call.

"Well, shit, that ain't much," Brugal muttered.

"It bigger than anything we've got here, and you don't want to be on the receiving end of it. Besides, it'll be the soldiers inside that ship, their helos and landing craft, not to mention their tanks, that'll be their main weapons," Holleran told him.

Another round was fired, this time evidently missing the building as an explosion was heard beyond the town and from the jungle to the north.

"Uh, how many landing craft do they have, Holleran?" Jay asked, eyes snapped onto the distant ship.

"I think four of the LCACs. Maybe more of some smaller boats."

"I think I see all four of them, then," he told him, watching four separate hovercraft disgorge from the back of the ship.

"I think their LCACs are smaller than ours, so each one might carry 25 or 30 troops, less if they are carrying any armor. Can you see if there are tanks on them?"

"No, not yet. LCpl Maus, report this to Capt Niimoto. Let him know what's coming, if he can't see for himself," Jay ordered.

He could hear Maus in the background, reporting the LCACs, but his attention was focused on the landing craft as they wheeled around for a moment before oriented towards the shore. It was only then that he could see that two of the landing craft had tanks on board.

"Maus, let them know that there are two tanks inbound, on the first and the third LCAC, the first being the one on the eastern end of their line."

He could see a couple more conventional boats take to the water, but they would be some time to make it ashore. He barely registered another round whistling by the control tower to impact once again on the city office building.

The LCACs were picking up speed, heading towards the shore. It looked like they were going to hit the low seawall that made up the southern edge of the island. It made sense, given the dense jungle and rocks that protected the rest of the island, but that also meant that if the air cushion landing craft could clear the seawall, they would have to cross the runway out in the open. If they didn't have the clearance to make it over the seawall and up on land, they would have to debark their pax right there, and the Chinese soldiers would have to rush over close to 175 meters of open ground to close with the Marines in the tree line.

The 60mm mortars below him and up against the tree line were zeroed in on the seawall, so Jay asked Holleran to shout down to them to get ready. He would have the corporal adjust fire as he could, but hitting a moving target when the rounds were in the air for 45 seconds was a difficult proposition. They had a wire running down to the mortar section, but using that could block someone else who needed it, and it was just as easy, if not easier, to simply shout out the adjustments.

As the LCACs were about halfway to the shore, three large helos lifted off the flight deck of the ship. The Chinese ship was not like the *Makin Island* with a large flight deck. It was more like an older American LPD, but with a smaller flight deck and from the way the ship had been angled towards the shore, Jay hadn't seen the three helos. There was no mistaking them now, though. They looked something like the Marines' Sea Stallions, so they probably had a good-sized troop-carrying capacity.

"Maus," he shouted out, "Let them know we've got three large helos inbound!"

He tried to remember just what weapons the rifle company had that could bring down a helo. He knew they didn't have any anti-aircraft missiles. The one anti-aircraft team with the MEU had gone to Taiping Island. A SMAW II Serpent could bring one down, and the Weapons Platoon Assault Section had three Serpent teams. Hitting a fast-moving helo with one would be difficult, though.

They didn't have any Javelins, the longer-range anti-armor missile, due to a manufacturer backlog, but the lighter Predator SRAW, which Jay had seen with least one team of gunners, would take down a tank, much less a helo.

Two helos pulled off to the west, making a long loop away from the southern side of the island. One helo came right towards the beach, following the LCACs in trace.

Something caught the corner of Jay's eyes to the right, not through his bino's lenses, and for a moment, he thought the Chinese had gotten a helo in without anyone noticing it. He pulled back the binos to see the Osprey taking off down from the boat basin. It looked good to see it, but the Chinese must have seen it too while it was moving into position. The next round from the ship's gun almost immediately impacted down in that direction, so that answered that question.

The Osprey quickly moved from helo to plane configuration, turned away from the line of incoming LCACs, the started to loop back, getting itself in line for a run. All of the LCACs immediately opened up with some sort of machine gun fire, but the Osprey was moving quickly into the attack. Its minigun opened up, firing on each of the Chinese landing craft which had been conveniently in a line.

Jay could see the rounds impacting on the LCAC's, now about 700 to 800 meters offshore, and sending up geysers of water in between each vessel. The second LCAC from the east suddenly swerved, whether because of damage or to try and avoid the Osprey's withering fire, Jay wasn't sure, and it almost collided with the first LCAC in line.

The Osprey reached the end of the line and started banking hard. It was still airborne despite all the rounds thrown its way. It looked like it was going to come back for another run.

The Chinese helo, though, jumped forward like a hornet, flashes from a large gun spitting fire out its side. In a moment, Jay could hear the reports. It had to be at least a 20mm cannon. One round could bring down the Marine plane.

The Osprey reversed the bank, pulling it away from the line of tracer fire reaching out to it. The pilot came back towards the beach, then kept banking until he had his plane facing back out. He went back into the attack, the LCACs starting to commence firing again as he got close.

Jay couldn't believe it. He had heard of troops in the trenches of WWI stopping to watch the dogfights, but a dogfight between an Osprey and a Chinese transport helo? It was pretty surreal.

There was a boom coming from the runway. Two Marines had run out and had launched a Predator SRAW out towards the LCACs. The missile quickly closed the distance and impacted on one of the LCACs. Jay expected to see a huge explosion, but the LCAC kept advancing.

The Chinese helo, though, evidently only had one cannon, and it was window-mounted. It had gotten itself out of position to use it and had slowed down to pivot, to get its gun facing the Osprey that was zooming in, its own minigun ablaze.

That was its fatal error. The Osprey's minigun was not designed for air-to-air fighting, but by slowing down, the Chinese helo made it an easy target for the Marine plane, and the minigun found its mark. The helo exploded into flames and plunged into the water 300 meters below.

Cheers erupted in the control tower as they high-fived each other. Jay couldn't believe what he had just seen. That captain had just managed to do something amazing.

The Osprey pulled back and started to bank again. But that exposed its belly to the Chinese ship, maybe 2 klicks further out. It was only then that Jay noticed the flashes that indicated the ship was firing with some sort of heavy automatic weapon. When the Osprey suddenly lurched, he knew the Chinese gunners on the ship had hit their mark as well.

The big bird faltered in the air, then began to lose altitude quickly. Jay could just make out the propellers starting to rotate into helo-mode. Maybe the pilot was trying to get the plane to auto-rotate. There wasn't any time, though. With a splash, the Osprey hit the water hard, parts breaking off and flying back up through the air.

His team fell silent. From the heights of joy, they had plummeted into the depths. No one said a word.

Jay looked back out to take in the whole scene. One LCAC, the first one, was on fire and evidently sinking. But the other three were continuing on, one slower than the other two, but still advancing. Explosions were sounding in the trees below as the ship's 3 incher opened up, but it would not be having any effect on the Marines in the tree line. The ship was overshooting them.

Off to the west, in the distance, the other two helos were mere specks. Jay wasn't sure what they were up to.

"OK, that's that. Let's get back to work, guys," he said. "Cpl Holleran, tell the mortars to prepare for targets 15 and 17. We'll give the order to fire. If the LCACs shift and land to the side of where they are lining up now, they have to be ready to shift, too."

The Marines below him were holding their fire. Seeing that the Predator SRAW had little effect on the LCAC, he doubted they would waste any more of the precious missiles. They would probably wait until they had a more appropriate target.

He looked around. The control tower was a little crowded, and there was no reason to put everyone in such a vulnerable position.

"Wellington, Brugal, and Cpl Destafney, I want you to climb on down. Cpl Destafney, if anything happens here, I want you to get to where you can observe the best you can and keep reporting."

He needed Cpl Holleran, but he was tempted to send LCpl Maus down as well. However, he knew he might need a runner, so he kept him. With the others climbing down the ladder, that left the three of them in the tower. That was enough to do the job.

"OK, Mark, fire off the mortars."

Cpl Holleran yelled down to the mortar section where Marines were at the ready. They released the rounds, then quickly picked up the next round and sent them after the first. Six rounds were now in the air.

One of the approaching LCACs actually picked up speed as it tried to flow over the seawall. It didn't make it. With a crash, it shuddered to a stop. Jay hadn't been sure if the wall was high enough to form a barrier, but evidently it was beyond the smaller Chinese LCACs' capabilities. Another LCAC slowed down to a stop, then let its ramp down. Jay was blocked from seeing how well the ramp reached onto the land, but a puff of black smoke from the tank onboard indicated it was good enough. He could just see the top of the tank begin to move when the mortar rounds hit.

Four rounds hit on the runway. As the runway was seven or eight feet above the low tide, they had no effect on the Chinese. Another round probably hit the water as Jay never saw an impact.

The sixth round, though, somehow hit inside the LCAC that had tried to breach the seawall.

A 60mm mortar round is not the most devastating round in the world, but in the confines of a cargo baby, the effect was magnified. Jay could imagine the carnage inside.

Cpl Holleran was already giving corrections to the mortar section when the damaged LCAC pulled back, then slowly turned around. It didn't look like any troops had gotten off. A mortar would have a hard time putting an LCAC out of commission, but it could certainly take out its passengers.

Two landing craft, though, had been able to debark their passengers, and there was a tank on shore. Firing began to come from the Marines, forcing the Chinese to hug the small area between the seawall and the edge of the runway, but some of them began to fire back.

"Mark, let's get some rounds on deck. Maus, let Kilo know that there are approximately 50 Chinese ashore and one tank. I think they've got two heavy machine guns as well."

The familiar incoming whistle and explosion made him jump. *Why had they shifted their fire?* he wondered.

The increasing louder whup-whup-whup of an incoming helo answered that question. Spinning around, he could see one of the Chinese helos bearing down on them from the north. Another one was further to the north, looking like it was doing the Chinese version of a fast-rope insertion, but the one bearing down on him took his undivided attention.

"Incoming!" he shouted down to the mortar team and the lone machine gun team with them.

"Incoming" might be more appropriate for incoming rounds, not helos, but it got the point across.

The machine gunner spun around and started firing, but only got off a burst of maybe six or seven rounds when his weapon jammed. Jay stepped out the back hatch and onto the railing, firing his M4. He could see the rounds impacting on the canopy of the helo, now only 40 meters away and a bit higher, but they were having no effect. His small caliber rounds could not penetrate the glass.

The pilot pointed straight at him, and Jay could clearly see him turn his head and say something to the co-pilot. He knew if that bird had a belly-mounted gun, he would have been toast.

He quit firing, pulling down Maus' weapon as well. No use wasting ammo. They were going to need all their rounds when the helo disgorged 25 or 30 angry Chinese soldiers.

He looked back to see if the machine gun team had cleared their weapon. They were fervently working on it, it seemed, but Jay didn't have much hope that they could get it working in time.

One Marine, though, was running up to the helo, not away from it. He carried a mortar tube and baseplate, holding it in front of him like some sort of personal weapon. The mortar could be fired in the handheld mode, but what he expected to do with it, Jay wasn't sure. The mortar was not made to be a direct fire weapon. If he managed to fire it directly at ground troops and not hit the ground first, Jay wasn't even sure the round would arm.

As he got closer, Jay recognized the Marine, LCpl Francisco Diaz. He and Diaz had spoken a few times on the ship. Diaz wanted to go recon, and Jay had given him what he needed to do to prepare himself.

LCpl Diaz stopped about 30 meters to the west of the control tower. He calmly knelt, using his hands to hold the mortar in place. His hand reached down to the trigger, and all became clear. The M224 mortar was usually fired by dropping a round down the chamber. The firing pin would set off the propellant, and the round would take off. However, the mortar also had a trigger. A round could be placed in the tube, and when the trigger was pulled, the round would then launch.

One hand on the tube to aim it, the other on the trigger, Diaz intended to put a round into the helo. Jay glanced back for a moment, and he could see the co-pilot had obviously realized the same thing. But Diaz was at the forward quarter of the helo, and he was effectively masked from any of its weapons. The pilots began to rotate the helo just as ropes fell out the back, probably trying to get their side-door cannon to bear.

The cannon started firing, explosions beginning to walk their way to Diaz as the helo came about. As the bird rotated, Jay saw a Chinese soldier on one of the ropes, but holding on as the bird moved.

Come on, shoot! Jay silently implored as Diaz just knelt there, slightly adjusting the angle of the tube.

A cannon round exploded about 10 meters from him. Then, with what looked to be a nod, LCpl Diaz squeezed the trigger.

There was the familiar soft, hollow-sounding chuff as the round took off, and Jay was sure he could actually see the round as it flew past the control tower and impacted into the side of the helo, penetrating it before detonating. An explosion literally tore out the side of the bird, parts flying, some of those parts even impacting on the side of the control tower.

Almost in slow motion, the bird turned over and fell, slamming into the ground on its side. The props tried to turn a few more times, but they flew into pieces as the ground broke them up. The helo bounced once, then broke apart into two huge chunks, the front section on fire.

The soldier who had been on the rope had somehow escaped intact. He jumped off the ground and began to run, but right at the mortar section instead of away from it. Jay didn't even have to fire as the soldier was quickly cut down. A few more soldiers stumbled out the back of the helo, collapsing on the ground. One soldier crawled, or tried, to, that is. He fell still, whether from being shot or from the crash, Jay wasn't sure.

Another incoming round from the ship bounced off the roof of the control tower, somehow not detonating. He didn't know if the pilots had comm with their ship and had requested the fire, or if it was just their turn on the firing list.

"Mark, Maus, get the hell off of here!"

LCpl Maus had just put his feet on the ladder when another round came in, hitting the base of the tower. The explosion threw shrapnel up, one piece hitting Jay in the cheek. He reached up to see how badly he had been hit when the tower began to lean.

"Oh, shit," he heard LCpl Maus say as the tower began its long fall to the ground.

Jay watched the ground rush up before all went dark.

Chapter 33
Pagasa Island

When the first round exploded in the trees about 50 meters off to the left, most of the Filipinos hit the deck. The trees were dense enough so that no shrapnel made it that far, but it was still disconcerting.

Pete didn't think they were being targeted by the Chinese. There was no reason to do so as they had a much bigger threat with Kilo Company. The island was pretty flat, and with naval gunfire, errors in range would be the norm. Still, rounds that were overshot or on target had the same effect if they fell among you.

When under indirect fire, the rule of thumb was to disperse, but Pete feared losing control if they did that in the dense jungle. The matter was taken out of his hands, though, when a voice in back of him shouted out something in Tagalog, and people started scrambling up and pushing into the trees on either side of the path. Pete was losing control whether he wanted to or not.

He started to call everyone back when another round hit off to the left, closer this time. People started crashing forward, eager to get to the north and to the rendezvous point, a large rock on the shore that had enough deep water on the sea side of it that boats could come alongside.

Instead of trying to round everyone back to the path, he motioned to his Marines to spread out and try and cover what was now essentially a mass of people on line and moving forward. He stayed on the path himself, along with Analiza and two other Filipinos, trying to maintain contact with the people on either side of him. He didn't like the arrangement and felt somewhat helpless, but they knew where they were going. This was virgin territory to him.

Analiza touched his shoulder, catching his attention, and said, "Don't worry. We've all been to Bird Rock. We know the way. Everyone'll get there."

"I don't know. What if we run into the Chinese? I can't protect everyone when they're spread out like this."

"If they come, they come. But I don't think they'll be anxious to go digging around in the bush. Do you?"

"I guess that's a good point," he conceded.

He continued to move north with his three charges. He could see a few people on either side of him and could hear more crashing through the vegetation and occasionally calling out.

The path, such as it was, got even smaller and less distinct. If the townspeople knew how to get to Bird Rock, they certainly did not make the trip often, if the path was any indication. Branches tore at him, one raising a stinging welt on his face. He brought his visor down. None of the electronics worked, so he couldn't see his display, and while with it down he was hotter, at least his face was protected from the braches and vines.

As he trudged forward, he heard the whup-whup of a helo. For a moment, he thought the *Makin Island* was finally within range and had sent its helos to evacuate the civilians, but when he caught a quick glimpse of the helo through the low trees, he knew it wasn't American. Olive grey, the yellow-outlined red star and bar at the base of the tail assembly gave it away. It was Chinese.

Pete should have figured that the Chinese were not going to simply rely on a frontal assault, attacking on the Marines' terms. Like anyone else, they would want to adjust the battlefield to give them an advantage. What they probably didn't realize was just how thick the jungle was. As the helo was flying north, the more distance it put between wherever troops would be inserted and Kilo Company, the longer it would take for them to be an influence in the battle.

Of course, as the helo was north of his position, if the Chinese were going to move south to join the battle, they would have to go through his Marines and the Filipinos. He wished he could inform Kilo of what was happening. Sgt McNamara, though, was in the control tower, and surely he could see the Chinese helo. He would get the word to Tony.

The sound of the helo was not receding, and Pete realized that it must be hovering up ahead, possibly debarking troops, either by rappelling or fast-rope, if the Chinese even had that capability. Pete wished he had studied the Chinese PLA in more detail. Knowing what they could and couldn't do would be a help.

If Chinese troops were being inserted 100 or 150 meter ahead, then he wanted the Filipinos out of the way. He ran off to the left first, then back across the path and to the right, telling those on either side of him to move further away from the path, then to hunker down and stay out-of-sight. He now wished he had kept everyone better under his control, but it was too late for that. He asked those nearest the path to pass the word to those further out, and to pass the word that he wanted Gunny Sloan.

He could hear the word going further out. The good thing was that in this vegetation, someone could pass within five feet of someone else and not see him or her. That was great for the Filipinos, but he had seven Marines with him, and he wasn't sure whether simply protecting the Filipinos as he was ordered trumped doing something about the Chinese soldiers who were probably ahead of him

He had to see what was happening. He probably should wait for the gunny, but waiting could take the initiative out of his hand.

Turning to Analiza, he told her, "Stay here. When my gunny gets here, tell him to wait. I'll be back in a moment."

She looked like she wanted to argue, but she seemed to accept it and nodded, kneeling down under a gnarled tree of some sort.

Pete slowly pushed forward along the path, senses on high alert. If there even were Chinese soldiers on that hello, it sounded like they would have had been inserted only a short distance away. If they were there, he didn't know what their mission was, which way they were going, or how many there were. On the plus side, they probably wouldn't be expecting anyone to be out here in the middle of the jungle, a good 500 meters from the northern shoreline.

He looked back along the path. He was probably only 30 meters from where he had left Analiza and the others, but it felt like he was completely alone. He knew he should get back, or at least wait for the rest of his team, but he wanted to get just a bit further in order to see if in fact there was anyone in their path.

Stepping carefully, he moved forward another 10 meters to where a dense stand of some sort of tall, bamboo-like grass formed a barrier just off the path. Although it was only about a dozen feet high or so, it was a good four feet wide and so tightly packed as to act as sort of a pseudo-tree trunk. He had no idea what would cause it to grow that way, but it would give him some cover from which he could try and see if there was anyone in front of them.

In back of him, he could hear nothing. His charges were either silent or the jungle too dense for sound to travel far. In front of him was also silent. Even the sounds of explosions off in the distance seemed muted in the humid, oppressive heat.

He really should not be alone, and he knew he needed to get back. But first, he wanted to look down the path to see if there was any sign of the Chinese. He pulled out his K-Bar, then very slowly, he moved to the edge of the stand of tropical grass and carefully cut a few loose leaves that came off the main stalks and were blocking the view forward. The leaves fell silently to the ground, and he carefully peered around the big stalks.

The kick caught him right across the face. His helmet shield was designed as a both a screen on which his tactical information could be displayed as well as to protect him from fire and offer some degree of protection from shrapnel. It was not designed to absorb the full impact of a kick.

The faceshield was driven back into his face, smashing his nose, but the force of the kick was spread out over a larger area than had the PLA soldier's kick directly contacted him across his face. Pete was knocked to the ground, and his weapon went flying back into the bushes.

Surprised, his nose aflame, but not really stunned, he grabbed the K-Bar, which had fallen beside him, and jumped up. The PLA soldier was in mid-jump doing some sort of flying back kick.

Pete had received not only the normal Marine MCMAP hand-to-hand combat training but also advanced training as a member of Recon. However, in the split second when he saw that booted foot coming his way, none of that training came into play, and instinct simply took over. He ducked while raising his hand, the one with the knife in it.

Instead of impacting on Pete's head, the soldier's leg impacted on the knife at the lower calf, just above his boot. While the kick was jarring, most of the force of the kick drove the knife deeper into the soldier's flesh where it essentially rode up his fibula, slicing his calf as clean as if a butcher might have done. The K-Bar rode up to the soldier's knee where his momentum knocked the knife out of Pete's hand.

The soldier fell to the ground, grasping at his leg which was spouting a bright crimson fountain. It was then that Pete saw the rifle slung across the soldier's back. Why the soldier had decided to go Kung Fu on him or why he was out on the path alone were questions that flashed through Pete's mind as he reached down to draw his Colt. His right hand was numb from the kick, so he had to transfer the .45 to his left hand. But at this range, which hand he used didn't matter. The soldier was in bad shape and had only a moment to try and reach around to his rifle when Pete fired two rounds into his chest. Without body armor, the rounds made a messy work of him.

With the two rounds breaking the silence, shouts sounded in front of him, foreign shouts. A burst of rounds came flying from down the path. Pete would swear later that the rounds sounded like bees going past his ear as he dove back behind the stand of grass, scrambling to get his rifle. His right hand was still numb, but he needed that M4.

He could hear the several sets of footsteps running as his left hand closed on his rifle and he struggled to swing around and face his enemies. He knew he wasn't going to make it, but he had to try.

Another burst of fire in back of him opened up, and he turned to see one PLA soldier fall on the path, the upper part of his body flopping past the stand of grass to lie just two feet from him. Pete looked back to see Gunny Sloan and LCpl Viejes charging down the path, rifles a blazing.

"Come on, sir!" his gunny shouted, pulling him up.

Pete didn't need any encouragement. Together, the three Marines sprinted back down the path.

When they saw Cpl Schmidt at the side of the path, weapon at the ready, they dived off the path and into the jungle.

"Are you an idiot, Lieutenant? That was a pretty fucking stupid thing to do!" Gunny Sloan shouted, his anger evident.

1stLt Peter Van Slyke didn't have a comeback to his platoon sergeant. The Gunny was absolutely right.

Chapter 34
Pagasa Island

Sgt Steptoe felt the pressure of the explosion, his breath knocked out of him. The Chinese rocket had been their most deadly weapon, killing and wounding wherever it was on target. This one, thankfully, had detonated in back of their lines, so he didn't think anyone had been taken out by it.

The fight, so far, was not like anything that he would have imagined. Both of his prior experiences in combat had been more fast-paced, more frantic action at times. Here, faced with a professional army, things had bogged down. He still wasn't sure how many Chinese soldiers were on the back side of the runway, a mere 175 meters away from him, but the LCACs and a few smaller boats had made several trips from the offshore ship.

About 20 minutes after the first Chinese landed, they had attempted an assault, spearheaded by their lone light tank. The blue tank was almost immediately taken out by a Predator SRAW fired from somewhere to his right, and with a heavy pounding of machine gun fire and mortars, the assault quickly fizzled out, sending the soldiers, in their odd blue-toned camouflaged uniforms, fleeing back to their side of the battlefield, leaving the burning hulk and four bodies on the runway.

Since then, the ship continued to fire its lone gun, but its effect was minimal. The rounds either hit on the runway, some actually skipping back up into the air, or hit long. The Chinese had some sort of grenade launcher, and they fired the occasional harassing fire, but these two caused only minor injuries to legs or arms, nothing life-threatening so far.

One sniper had tried to stick his head up above the edge of the seawall, but a quick burst from an IAR sent him flying back in a haze of blood.

The rockets, though, were a different story. The Chinese soldiers weren't even aiming the shoulder-launched weapon. A soldier would pop up and fire, the rocket blasting across the runway to explode in the air above the Marines. The rocket housed a fuel-air warhead, and the blast, while not huge, was deadly. It blew down the short trees that gave them cover and killed and maimed the Marines in its blast radius. Already, four rounds had been on target, killing 9 Marines and seriously wounding another seven. What surprised Steptoe was that one rocket had exploded at the far left of the Marine's line where it married up with the Filipino soldiers. The Filipinos, without body armor, fared better than the Marines. Two Marines, Pvt Dexter and LCpl Alaman, had been killed while the Filipinos next to them had only been injured.

Luckily, the Chinese didn't seem to have too many of them. Or at least, they had not fired too many. Steptoe hoped that was because of supply, not because they were saving them for an all-out assault.

Meanwhile, the mortar section continued to rain down rounds on the Chinese positions. They were quite low on ammo, so the tempo had slowed, but hopefully, the firing was enough to keep the Chinese occupied.

Steptoe was still amazed that someone had managed to take down a Chinese helo with a mortar round. That was one for the books.

There was still one helo in operation. It had tried to make a gun run on their position, but a Predator SRAW fired at it made it pull off, even if the shot had missed. They could barely make out the helo on the flight deck of the Chinese ship.

The Filipino soldiers had made one mini-assault. Positioned at the far left of the Marine line at the boat basin, they had maneuvered forward in the rocks and in knee deep water to the very edge of the southeast corner of the runway, popping out to fire down the line of Chinese before pulling back. The Filipino lieutenant reported killing at least 15 Chinese, but Capt Niimoto thought that was probably more hopeful than fact. The assault, though, forced the Chinese to spend manpower to refuse that flank.

The skipper and the XO had discussed the possibility of assaulting the Chinese and throwing them off the island, but the same runway that kept the Chinese from successfully assaulting would prove devastating to them as well. Steptoe could see the skipper was frustrated. He didn't want to sit there as targets for the shoulder-launched rockets, but to attack would be foolhardy. Their best bets were either to egg the Chinese into a frontal assault that they could beat back or just hang on until the *Makin Island* was within range. Just one Cobra II run down the Chinese line would be devastating. Of course, a strike from the carrier group would be appreciated as well.

The best the skipper could figure was that they could expect something in another three hours or so—that is, if things were quiet on Taiping and they received all available support.

Sgt Steptoe took a deep breath. That last blast had been a little close for comfort. Whatever the Chinese were using as a fuze was less than 100% accurate, something for which he was eternally grateful. If it had detonated another 25 or 30 meters closer, that might have been all she wrote for Mrs. Steptoe's favorite son.

Over his ringing ears, he heard the land line, which was still somehow functioning, buzz. He picked up the handset.

"This is Three. We've got an incoming Osprey, over."

"Wait one, over," Steptoe told him.

"Hey skipper, Third Platoon's got an Osprey inbound," he shouted over the five meters to where the company commander was prone and talking with the first sergeant.

"Tell them to pop the red smoke. We don't want him landing in the middle of this. He won't have a chance. With the smoke and that big target out there, he should get the message and get back to the MEU. Hopefully, he'll come back with a few of his friends," the captain told him.

"Three, pop a red smoke. We don't want him to try to land, over," Steptoe spoke into his handset.

"Roger. I think he's already figured it out. He's circling well off shore, but we are popping smoke, out."

There was a short delay, then down the runway, a good 500 meters away, red smoke started to form, to be wisped away in the slight breeze. Steptoe looked at his watch. If the Osprey could get back to the *Makin Island* in, say 45 minutes, and reported what was happening, then maybe they could have some help here in about 2 to 3 hours, just like the skipper said.

"Stand by," came a shout from down the line.

The Chinese must have seen the Osprey as there was a flurry of activity. A puff of black smoke indicated where the light tank had started back up. They could hear shouts as the Chinese got organized for something.

When nothing happened for a few minutes, Steptoe started to relax a bit. That was premature.

Two tanks, not just the one Steptoe knew was there, crested the edge of the runway as five separate rockets were fired into the Marine lines and what looked to be 100 soldiers came "over the top," firing as they came. Three SMAW II Serpents and one Predator SRAW reached out to the armor, two rounds hitting one tank and stopping it cold. The other tank kept coming as the Chinese rockets exploded over the Marines.

Captain Niimoto was on the handset, yelling out orders, so Steptoe kept watch forward, acting as the skipper's security. The headquarters element might normally have been back further, but the dense vegetation would have kept them in the dark as to what was going on, so they were right up on the line.

Just to his right, LCpl Hanks stood up with his SMAW, trying to get a better shot at the tank that was spraying fire at the Marines. He calmly lined up his sights, then sent a spotting round downrange.

Shoot the rocket! Steptoe silently implored.

But Hanks took too long. The tank had spotted him, and with one round, hit him dead on. Steptoe was watching as the Marine simply came apart.

The blast knocked Steptoe, rolling him over onto his back. His hearing was gone, blasted away. Blood was running down his left arm, but he flexed it without problem. He rolled back over, and the tank was now only 40 meters or so from the tree line.

A frontal assault over a runway seemed stupid, but if they could keep the heads of the Marines down, Steptoe knew it could work. They could penetrate the line, then roll up the sides. First Platoon had been sent back once firing had been heard to the north of the town to protect their rear, and they couldn't get back in time to support the other two platoons if things got dire.

Right in front of him, a few feet into the open, LCpl Hanks' arm lay, the hand looking normal. Steptoe's attention was drawn to the fingernails and the half-moon of dirt under each one. In his daze, he found himself thinking that Hanks should have kept them clean.

Beyond Hanks' arm, the SMAW lay, looking basically whole. Steptoe was dazed, but he knew he should get the weapon. He got to his knees and crawled out, stopping to carefully move Hanks' arm aside, then continuing to the SMAW. He sat down and cradled the weapon.

Sgt Steptoe was not a SMAW gunner. He was a communicator. But as the saying went, "Every Marine is a rifleman." He knew how to operate a SMAW, even if he had never fired a real one, only a simulator. His thinking wasn't clear, but rote training took over.

He checked the optics. If they were smashed, the weapon would be essentially useless. But the SMAW II Serpent was designed with a roll cage over the optics, and in this case, the roll cage had done as it was designed, protecting them.

Sgt Steptoe swung his legs around, still sitting, going through the steps in firing the weapon, just like he was on the range back at Pendleton. Place the safety on fire. Check, Hanks had already done that. Pull the charging handle. Check. Hanks had done that, too. He inspected the spotting rifle magazine, which looked dented. He decided to skip using it. The range was minimal, after all. He checked the sights one more time. They were set for "HE" and 100 meters. He hoped the round was something a little more effective against armor, but it was too late to worry about that.

Turning the range drum to 50 meters, he looked back and yelled out "Back blast area clear!"

Whether it actually was clear or not, he wasn't exactly sure given his foggy brain. He sighted in on the tank, which was traversing both its machine gun and main gun along the tree line. It was a light tank, but it looked huge in his sights. He was close enough that the patchwork light blue digital camouflage squares made it stand out more, giving him a specific point of aim. He calmly depressed the launch lever and pulled the trigger, sending the rocket straight into the side of the tank.

Evidently, the round had not been HE but either HEDP or HEAA, probably the later as the resultant explosion sent the turret of the tank spinning end over end and at least 30 feet into the air. Steptoe stared at the burning tank until something slammed into his chest. Gasping for breath seemed to clear his head. He had been hit, but a quick check showed that his armor had stopped the round. He might have a broken rib, but that was a small price to pay. He scrambled back into the tree line and into the shallow fighting position he had scraped out earlier.

The skipper was still yelling over the handset, but he gave Steptoe a thumbs up. His head clearing and his hearing coming back, he felt a tremor coming over him. He couldn't believe he had just taken on a tank and survived.

He tried to take a deep breath, but that brought on a spasm of pain from his bruised or broken ribs. Looking out over the killing field, the Chinese attack had petered out. With both tanks gone, the infantry had retreated, but not without leaving bodies scattered on the crushed coral runway. One soldier was only 20 meters in front of him, slowly and painfully trying to crawl back, leaving a bright red trail of blood. He was in full sight of the Marines, but they were content to let him go. If he managed the long crawl back, dragging useless legs, well, he was no longer a threat to anyone, and an able-bodied soldier would have to take the time to give him aid.

As the firing died down, reports started coming in. The Chinese attack, although beaten back, had been devastating. Third Platoon had taken the brunt of the attack, and they had lost 8 Marines killed, including 1stLt Gaines. Another 11 had been wounded. Second Platoon had lost four Marines with eight wounded. Doc Parker had been one of those killed, so the skipper sent Doc Sanjay, the senior corpsman, to take care of them. The Filipinos had been the only ones to escape serious injury.

Technically, this was a victory. But another such victory might be their last. They just didn't have the manpower to stand up to another major assault.

Chapter 35

Aboard the Jinggan Shan

Captain Teng Huang-fu was livid. That idiot, Major Lim, had actually gone into the attack, spooked by the American tilt-rotor that had made a brief appearance. He had obviously been concerned that it would make a gun run on his troops, but couldn't he see that the plane had turned back?

Communications with the PLA Marines on the ground was still spotty, but he had watched the attack through his big eyes on his bridge wing. Now, instead of three tanks on shore, he had none. He had no armored personnel carriers, no artillery. He had possibly 70 effectives on shore and another 800 still onboard his ship. The main issue was getting those 800 on shore where they could roll over the American soldiers.

From the beginning, this operation had been plagued with mismanagement and bad luck. Initially, the two ships had set out with half a brigade of Marines for a scheduled exercise. When this contingency had come up, instead of pulling back into port to better prepare, they had been sent as is to dislodge the American invaders.

So instead of being combat-loaded, they didn't have enough ammunition or even the right types, they only had the ship's three Z-8 helos with no attack helos, and they had only 6 light amphibious tanks and 6 armored personnel carriers.

Even the ship's 3-inch gun was less than effective. Thitu was very flat, and while the gun was accurate in deflection, the slightest error in aiming or roll of the ship could send the round quite short or quite long. The gun was quite effective in protection from smaller ships or in sinking a Somali or Malayan pirate, but against troops, it was only minimally useful.

Then the cursed American tilt-rotor had taken out not only one of his LCACs but one of his Z-8s as well. Another LCAC had been damaged and was being hurriedly repaired, and a second Z-8 had been destroyed somehow back near the island's town.

The only good thing was that they had more than the normal 750-man Marine battalion on board. With budget concerns and shortages of bunker oil, their training cruise had been expanded to get more Marines trained instead of just the normal single battalion.

Of course, the Marines could not fight from the ship. They had to get ashore. And for all the lip service the PLA gave to amphibious operations, they just didn't have the capability to put large numbers of Marines or soldiers ashore quickly.

He raised the big eyes a bit to take in the roofs of the town towards the middle of the island. On one building, the red flag of the People's Republic had been spread out on the roof. He wondered if this was a ruse, but he had to go on the assumption that the missing Chinese citizens were inside. As such, he had ordered the building not be targeted.

There was one other undercurrent that was weighing on Captain Teng's mind that increased his anger. When Senior Captain Chou had sent him on this mission, he had made certain comments, purposely, Teng was sure, that lead him to believe that this operation was not the simple rescue and retaliation operation he had been told it was, that this was part of a larger strategy.

Captain Teng would never question orders. If the command sent him to invade Los Angeles or Sydney, he would do it without question. But Captain Teng hated incompetence. And if this was a planned operation, why would they be sent in half-assed and half-armed? Why not provide air support? Why not go in so robust that nothing could stand in their way? It just didn't make sense.

"Sublieutenant Chin, how long for high tide?" he asked over his shoulder, eyes still glued to the beach.

"Two hours and 18 minutes," came back the immediate reply.

He didn't let it show, but he was pleased with Chin. The young officer was extremely competent and would go far in the PLA Navy.

He slowly backed away from the big eyes and looked at Lieutenant Colonel Huang, the Marine battalion commanding officer. He had left the Marine standing at attention for the last few minutes.

"Well, Lieutenant Colonel Huang, I hope you understand my orders," he said, keeping a steel edge to his voice.

"Yes, Captain Teng. I understand."

"No more glory-seeking? No more impromptu deviations from orders?"

"No Captain. We will follow your plan exactly."

Teng looked the Marine over. The PLA Marine Corps was the newest branch of the PLA, only reformed back in 1980 after being disbanded for almost 30 years. They were tough, he had to admit, in superb physical shape and used to extreme conditions. But sometimes their macho self-image got in the way of modern warfare. All PLA Marines were expert martial artists, for example, spending untold hours in hand-to-hand combat training. How that helped a tanker or an artilleryman, well, Captain Teng didn't know. Even an infantryman would be better served becoming an expert with his Type 95 Assault Rifle than learning how to break a brick with his hand.

This debacle was not totally the Marine commander's fault, though, he realized. It was the Navy, his own ship, that couldn't project the Marines' full force ashore. Well, that was going to change.

"I will allow you to lead the attack from the front, as you requested. I trust that you will succeed in your mission."

The Marine's chest actually swelled as he shouted out, "Thank you, captain. I will not fail you."

"It is not me you would be failing, but China. Now, go, get your troops ready."

Lieutenant Colonel Huang saluted, then did a perfect military about face before racing off.

One of the problems with the island was that the only reasonable place to conduct a landing was at the runway, and the seawall and foundation for the runway were just high enough that the LCACs could not clear the lip and get up on the land itself. Elsewhere, the rocks and jungle were too thick to enable any vessel to get ashore. However, to the west, over the same reef that still held the rusting hulk of a Filipino Navy ship that had run aground years ago, the vegetation near the shore was not quite as thick, certainly not thick enough to stop an LCAC from at least making it up to dry land. At high tide, there would be enough clearance for his remaining three LCACs and a few of his smaller boats to breach the outer reef and make it to shore. The vegetation was still too thick there to try and land tanks or armored personnel carriers, but it was feasible for the infantry Marines.

In addition to about 90 Marines in various launches and small boats available to him, and with the LCACs overloaded, he was going to land almost another 200 Marines in the LCACs on the west side of the island where they could roll up the American's flank. Supported by his remaining three tanks, which were already being ferried ashore to the south side of the runway, another 120 Marines already ashore and still arriving, and his lone helo, this would be more than enough to overwhelm the Americans. There wasn't any way they could resist.

Chapter 36
Zongnaihai, Beijing

General Chen Jun, Chief of Staff for the People's Liberation Army, walked down the hall of the party headquarters, his mind racing. He had just left the general secretary's office. When he had been summoned, he had assumed he was going to be sacked at best, at worst, well, that was better left unmentioned.

Instead, he had been ushered in with respect by the general secretary's staff and brought to the great man without delay. The general secretary even poured him tea.

Yu Deijang, the third-ranked vice premier was also there, smiling and asking about his wife and family. He asked General Chen to give his regards to his granddaughter on her birthday. Idle pleasantries took only a minute or so before the *raison d'être* for the meeting became clear. They wanted to know what he had planned to do about Taiping and Thitu.

This floored him. The People's Republic had made great pains to separate the PLA from any avenue of power. The PLA was an instrument of the Party, controlled by the Central Military Commission. Both men sipping tea with him were on that commission. For them to ask him with the deference they were showing was unusual, to say the least. In all the history of the nation, the CMC ordered, the PLA obeyed.

Not sure what they expected, he had spouted familiar party themes. They seemed to agree with him, but before he left, they made it clear that victory in the Wanli Shitang was vital to Chinese interests.

At least he now knew which way he was expected to jump. With this in mind, he was on his way out to return to PLA headquarters and give the order to General Li to use what resources he needed to finish the job at hand. Before he could get to security, though, Wang Jinping, the second-ranked vice premier personally stopped him in the hall.

"General Chen. It is good to see you here. I was about to call you, but as you are already here, perhaps we can go to my office and chat?"

"I would be honored, vice premier. Be assured, though, that the general secretary has already spoken to me about my duty."

"Ah, yes, the general secretary. Well, please humor me, if you will." The second-ranked vice premier held an arm out as if to escort the general.

General Chen shrugged. He wanted to get back and give the orders. Who knew what the Americans would do the longer this dragged out? But when the third most powerful man in the country asked for your presence, then who was he to say no?

Vice Premier Wang also asked about his granddaughter and her birthday. *Did the entire CMC keep tabs on his granddaughter?* he wondered.

They walked into the vice premier's spacious office. Sitting there, evidently waiting for them, were two more members of the CMC and another five members of the Politburo. This was a heavy meeting. General Chen wanted to assure them that he knew his duty, but years climbing the ranks in the PLA had given him a degree of political savvy. Sometimes, being astute meant keeping silent.

This group didn't waste time. As soon as the tea had been served, the vice premier got to business.

"General Chen, do you think the standard of living is better for our people now than it was, say 50 years ago?" the vice premier asked.

"Why certainly, sir, thanks to the Party and its leadership," came the rote answer.

"And why is that, general?"

"Well, because, well, ... the Party has led the people into prosperity."

"But how? What tools did they use?"

"We built up our manufacturing, our power."

"And who do we sell to, general? Who gets all those cars, machines, tools, electronics—all those things we make?"

"Why, the world does, vice premier," he replied.

"And who is our biggest trading partner?"

"The Americans are. They buy all our products."

"You are correct, General Chen. The Americans buy 22% of all Chinese exports. So I want to ask you, if we were at war with the Americans, how much of that 22% would they still buy?"

"Trade would be cut off, vice premier. They wouldn't buy anything."

"Exactly," Vice Premier Wang said, as if lecturing an undergraduate class. "And if the Japanese, the EU, the Russians, if they joined in a war, what would that do to trade?"

"I don't know the numbers, sir. But it would cut our trade."

"It would cut our trade by 76%, General Chen. That would plunge the country into recession. Inflation would take over, and that, as I am sure you are aware, would lead to civil unrest," he said, leaning back as if his point had been made.

"But Africa wouldn't join in a war, nor India," General Chen pointed out.

"We get raw materials from Africa, but as far as hard goods, they still do not buy much from us," Liang Chen-du, a younger member of the Politburo interjected, leaning forward in his seat, his round, soft face eager to make his point known.

General Chen sat back, his tea cooling and forgotten. He had thought his way forward was clear, but it was evident to him that this group of men did not want the conflict to continue. But why make their case to him? They needed to get together and decide amongst themselves, then just tell him what to do. This was not a military decision, after all. The military was merely the tool to implement the decision, whatever that may be.

"How would your granddaughter fare, general, if you could not provide for her, to buy her the things she wants in life?" the vice premier asked.

Was that an implied threat? he wondered. If so, that was not a smart thing to do. He was not without some power himself.

And then it hit him. Not only did he have *some* power, for the first time in the history of the nation, he had *the* power. With a united Party, with a united CMC, the PLA had no power. But the CMC, even the Party as a whole, was not united. There were two distinct factions, neither strong enough to overwhelm the other faction. The PLA, which had long been kept subservient to eliminate the chance of a coup, had the ability to shift the landscape, to put the power into one faction or the other. It could even take over, he realized, leading the way forward for the nation.

He settled back into his chair.

"Vice Premier Wang, my granddaughter would understand if she had to sacrifice. She would do what is right for China."

"Just as I am sure you will do the right thing for the nation, for our people. They have put their trust in you," the vice premier said, rising to shake his hand.

General Chen rose as well, and the two men shook.

What is right for China, Second-ranked Vice Premier Wang, may not match what you think is right, though, he thought before nodding at the others and leaving the office.

Chapter 37
Pagasa Island

Sergeant Harrington Steptoe had a wicked headache, and that bothered him much more than his aching ribs. He realized he probably had a concussion, but he didn't want to bother Doc Sanjay, who had some much more serious cases to attend. With Doc Parker among the dead, Doc Sanjay had his hands full trying to stabilize the seriously wounded. Some of them weren't going to make it unless help arrived right ricky-tick.

The skipper was trying to consolidate his forces. He had pulled two squads back from First Platoon, leaving only one squad and the mortar section to cover their rear. The odd bursts of fire from the north were proof enough that something was going on up there, and they could not afford to be surprised from that direction. With only five mortar rounds left, only one team was left as mortarmen—the other two teams became riflemen.

The two squads from First supplemented the decimated Third, but even then, the line was thin. The east side of the line, with Second and the Filipinos, was a little better off, but still, the distance between fighting positions was greater than what was recommended.

The ammo counts were trickling in, and the numbers weren't good. After redistribution, each Marine had about 9 rounds left. There was one SRAW Predator round, and the machine guns had less than 20 rounds apiece. The Chinese assaults had been turned back, but at a huge cost in ammunition, not even considering the more serious loss of life and limb. One more concerted effort by the Chinese and they would quickly be hand-to-hand.

Steptoe listened in to the skipper as the company headquarters and the platoon commanders discussed the situation.

He and Doc Sanjay were part of the headquarters, but Doc was off treating the wounded, and Steptoe was still somewhat dazed, so he was content to merely observe. The comm was pretty much set, anyway, with the wire and his three runners.

"Maybe we need to hit them first," the first sergeant said, straightening up a bit to glance over the runway.

"And cross that killing field?" the skipper asked. "That didn't serve them too well," he continued, pointing to the Chinese bodies that were beginning to bloat in the afternoon sun.

One tank was still on fire, the black smoke rising high into the air. The other two merely seemed abandoned as if they could be fired up and brought back into the attack. The one still on fire was the tank that Steptoe had taken out. It was close enough that he could smell the diesel and scorched hulk. It still seemed strange to think that he had somehow managed to kill the blue beast.

"You know we can't hold up much longer. And they keep bringing in more. If we can catch them on their offload, maybe we can knock out those damn LCACs," First Sergeant Davidson continued.

"I agree with you, Burke, but what're we going to knock them out with? A few grenades? And how're we going to get to them?" Capt Niimoto countered.

"What about around the end, like the Filipinos did?" he asked.

"I think they've got that covered now, First Sergeant," Lt Blumenthal put in. "Lieutenant Jones says the Chinese have a pretty strong force covering that flank now."

"Jones" did not sound like a typical Filipino name, but the Filipino lieutenant proved to be pretty competent, so Steptoe would be inclined to take his word on that. The skipper evidently shared the same opinion.

"I would love to take it to them. Just sitting here doesn't seem right, but in the defense, that's where we have the best chance at success. We just need to hold out until the MEU can reinforce us," the skipper said, glancing at his watch. "I think that can be as early as maybe 45 minutes?"

"I wish we could see what they're doing now," the XO said, peering through the trees and across the runway. "We think they have three tanks, right?"

"Yes, sir," Gunny Dailey responded.

"And we have only one SRAW, right?"

The gunny and the skipper nodded.

"So maybe we take out one tank, if we're lucky. That means there're two more. And that's when you want us to retreat, sir?"

The XO could be hot-blooded, to say the least. Steptoe never knew where he stood with the tall Wyoming Marine. He'd never been able to peg the man. And now he looked pretty upset.

"I wouldn't call it a retreat, Chael. The tanks can't follow us into the jungle, so by pulling back, we're going to force the Chinese to come after us on foot. And I don't think infantry to infantry that they can defeat us. Do you?" the skipper asked.

"Oh no, sir," the XO hurriedly responded. "It's just that, well, it just seems wrong to fall back in front of Chinese soldiers, sir."

"Falling back doesn't mean retreat," the first sergeant said. A moment ago, First Sergeant Davidson had been advocating an attack, but now he was onboard with pulling back. Steptoe didn't know if he had really embraced the skipper's plan or if he merely wanted to confront the XO. Neither man had ever seemed to fully accept the other, often vying for the skipper's attention. Steptoe thought it rather immature that they still brought that competition here when lives depended on professionalism.

Steptoe looked again to the Chinese position. They were less than 200 meters away, less than what every Marine fired on the rifle range. They could see the very tops of the three tanks, and there were furtive movements and quick glimpses of Chinese soldiers and they scurried about. It was surreal that they were so close, yet for the last 30 minutes or so, they seemed to be ignoring the Marines. Of course, it only seemed like they were ignoring them. They were building up their forces, and Steptoe was not looking forward to when they kicked off whatever it was they were planning. This was only the calm before the storm.

"November-Six-Tango, this is Sierra-Two-Whiskey, do you read me, over?"

It took a moment for Sgt Steptoe to realize that someone was trying to reach him over his radio. He had taken the radio off his back and stowed it in his fighting hole, just a piece of useless gear. He scrambled back to his hole, gasping from what that did to his ribs as he dove to reach the handset that he had wrapped around the harness.

"Kilo Company, come on, answer!" came another attempt, the operator throwing radio procedures out the window.

"This November-Six, um, this is Kilo Company, over!" he shouted into the handset.

"I've got them!" the voice came over, a little quieter as the operator--Sgt Bigby, it sounded like to Steptoe--spoke to someone else back on his end. "Kilo, look, you've got two Chinese cruise missiles inbound, impact in 90 seconds. These are the real thing. Take whatever cover you can, over."

Steptoe looked up to the others, but they had heard the message. All looked stunned.

"Uh, roger, over," he replied, routine taking over.

"Kilo Company, God be with you," came the simple response.

"Take cover, take cover!" the shout went out, making its way down the Marines' line.

Lt Blumenthal jumped up and rushed towards his platoon, echoing the warning.

"Well, I guess it was too good to be true, that this would be an infantry fight," the skipper said bitterly. "If they are committing cruise missiles, well, expect air strikes next if any of us survive."

"What do we do now, sir?" asked the XO, the edge of panic starting to creep into his voice.

"Not much we can do, lieutenant," the first sergeant answered calmly. "The Chinese cruise missiles pack a hell of a punch, enough to take out a carrier or an entire city block, and we're better off here and low, closer to their own troops." He craned his neck to look across the runway. "I wonder if they know they're screwed, too. No way they're going to be untouched."

Sgt Steptoe's ears were still ringing, but he became aware of a low rumbling from the north. He tried to look through the trees.

"Yea, that's them," the skipper confirmed.

He looked around at his headquarters. "It's been an honor, Marines, to serve with you. Semper fi."

There was no overt panic as the Marines came to grip with their fate. With their lines well over a kilometer long, some Marines would survive the strike, and maybe the mortar section and recon would escape unscathed, but any survivors would be easy pickings for the overwhelming might of the entire Chinese assault force. Even if some of those Chinese already ashore were casualties as well, they could already see the rotors of the helo on the far off ship turning on the deck while an LCAC started to emerge from the ship's well deck. Those would be the main landing force.

The approaching rumble became louder. Steptoe didn't realize you could hear your approaching death. He thought it would be more like the sequences shown on CNN or online, with death coming in silently. He guessed cruise missiles were either louder or slower than other forms of killing machines.

"Good work on that tank, Stepchild," Tony told him as the missiles began their final targeting.

They'd gone through a lot together. They'd both survived New Delhi when so many others hadn't. They both survived Somalia. Now, it looked like they would be going out together. It somehow seemed fitting.

Stepchild closed his eyes as the missiles reached them...then opened them again as both missiles continued on, out over the water.

He could clearly see the red star on both of them as the huge weapons flew on—they were definitely Chinese. He wondered for a second if they were going to turn back to get at them from a different angle, but the missiles ran true, right to the Chinese ship.

The twin explosions sent huge gouts of fire and smoke into the air. A moment later, the shock wave hit them. At more than three kilometers away, they witnessed the death of a ship.

Chapter 38
Pagasa Island

Pete took a deep drink of water, watching the Chinese Marines, he now knew them to be, load up on the big Chinese transport. It was hard to grasp that only the day before, they had been at each other's throats. Now, the disarmed Marines were calmly getting on board their aircraft to get out of there, guarded by only a dozen or so Filipino soldiers.

Pete had spent most of yesterday afternoon playing hide-and-seek with the Chinese Marines, the jungle too dense for real fighting. Other than the Chinese Marine he had killed, only one other Chinese Marine had been even hit, and on the American side, only Cpl Gutenev had been slightly injured, that from a branch going through a chunk of his thigh. None of the Filipinos had been injured.

When the Chinese cruise missiles had flown overhead, he hadn't known what was going on. Then Gunny Sloan's helmet comm had come to life, and in the resultant mish-mash of messages, he found out the Chinese ship had been destroyed. Pete had figured that the American forces had finally arrived, or maybe the *Mississippi* had discovered what was going on and had taken out the Chinese ship.

He was shocked to find out that the two missiles were Chinese. They had taken out their own ship.

The Chinese Marines on the island had received orders to surrender. Chael Shelton had told him later that evening that an angry Chinese major had followed a Chinese Marine carrying a white rag tied to a pole across the runway to be led to Tony Niimoto. With terse words, his eyes blazing, he had surrendered his Marines to the skipper, despite his greater numbers and three tanks.

Those three tanks, in their odd-looking blue digital camouflage, stood parked at the east end of the runway. Two Chinese crewmembers stood by each one, waiting for a Chinese transport to pick them up as well. Something was obviously up, but Pete didn't understand why the Chinese were being cut so much slack. They were the enemies, weren't they?

It had taken much longer for the 26 Chinese Marines facing him to surrender. They could hear the crackle of their radios, and even some yelling, but evidently, the Chinese were cautious. When Pete had been given the message from Kilo that the Chinese were surrendering, he had risked calling out into the jungle that he would accept their surrender. A few minutes later, a voice called out in broken English that they would be coming out, to hold their fire.

Pete had kept most of his Marines hidden, meeting the Chinese with only SSgt Tolbert and Cpl Schmidt. He had each Chinese Marine put his weapon on the deck before moving further back to his Marines. They didn't have any plastic wrist ties, so there was no way to restrain them. He had to trust that they really had surrendered.

The Chinese lieutenant had seemed upset when he saw the number of Marines Pete had, but he also seemed resigned. With some of the Filipinos picking up the Chinese weapons, he had a few more guards to escort the prisoners back to the town, and the Chinese sullenly, but without incident, let themselves be escorted out of the jungle.

The town was pretty damaged, the control tower down, and a still smoking hulk of a crashed helo lay on the ground. Pete's heart fell when he saw the tower, but he could not leave his prisoners to check on what happened to McNamara's team.

He marched the prisoners to the runway and handed them over, then rushed back to the town, not bothering to check in with the skipper. There were no bodies in the tower, so he ran over to the mortar section asking about McNamara. They pointed him to the community center, which had escaped unscathed.

Inside, he found McNamara and Maus being tended by one of Kilo's corpsmen. McNamara was conscious, but his back was probably broken. Maus had broken legs and an arm at the minimum. It was then that he learned that Cpl Holleran had not made it. He had been in the control tower when it had been hit, and he had not survived the fall.

This was the first of his Marines to die. He had seen other Marines die, even friends, and that had hit him, but this was different. Mark Holleran was one of HIS Marines. He had trained with him, he had lived with him. It hit him hard, and it took several minutes for him to gather himself.

The sounds of an aircraft made him jump, but it was an American Osprey, which made several passes and got confirmation over the radio that all was secure before landing. The most seriously wounded were lifted off the island and back to the *Makin Island* which had first gone to Taiping Island before being diverted to Thitu, or Pagasa Island, as the Filipinos kept telling him. An hour later, the first of the American helos arrived, bringing in supplies, more Marines, and taking off more of the wounded and dead. One of the helos brought in an MP team and the MEU XO, and they quickly took over the prisoners, allowing most of Kilo to get some rest.

By then, the Chinese ship had disappeared beneath the waves. When the *Makin Island* arrived offshore, there was no visible evidence that the Chinese ship had even been there.

An hour later, a Filipino C-130 landed, and about 100 Filipino soldiers ran out, looking ready for bear. They were commanded by a full colonel, and he wasted no time in taking charge of the island. He insisted on searching each Chinese Marine and soldier again, the PLA Army soldiers being the ones who had made the initial assault and who had been previously taken prisoner, but when he wanted to truss each prisoner like a turkey, the MEU XO, LtCol Ramsey, had intervened. Evidently, word had been passed down on how to treat the prisoners, and after some heated radio calls, probably back to the Filipino Army headquarters, the prisoners were left as they were and were fed and watered. The dead were treated with respect and covered with either white tarps or placed inside body bags.

When Pete saw how many Chinese had died, he had been surprised. There had to have been 200 bodies there waiting to be repatriated back to China. He knew Kilo Company had suffered pretty badly as well, but nowhere near that badly.

He had wondered which one of those covered bodies had been the Marine he had killed. He knew it could have been him, maybe should have been him. Why that young man had chosen to go hand-to-hand was beyond him. That decision had cost him his life. And that was why he was in a body bag, laying out on the runway, instead of himself.

While relieved that he had made it, even if banged up a bit, he didn't know what to feel. He was still angry about Cpl Holleran, angry that none of this had been necessary. And yes, he was confused as to why the Chinese were being treated so well. Oh, he wasn't advocating torture or retaliation, but why were they going home, even before the Marines were to be evacuated, was beyond him. He knew this was coming from on high, but it still rankled him. Those "on high" hadn't fought in this stinking jungle.

Getting a good meal and a good night's sleep had done wonders for his mood, though. Now, he was a little more detached as he watched the Chinese load the big transport.

"So,..." a soft voice said beside him.

He turned to see Analiza stepping up beside him.

"So," he responded, realizing how dumb that sounded.

"It seems strange to see them just leaving like this, like they are going home from a tour."

"I know what you mean," he replied.

They stood together for awhile, neither saying anything.

"How's your nose?" she asked, obviously searching for something to say.

He reached up to gingerly touch it before answering, "It hurts, and Doc says its probably broken, but there's no serious damage. They're going to look at it back on the ship."

With his other scars, a crooked nose, courtesy of the kick to his face by the now dead Chinese Marine, was the least of his worries.

"So, you'll be going back soon?" she asked.

Did he hear a hint of regret in the question?

"Yea," he looked at his watch before continuing, "in about two hours."

They were quiet for a moment before they both blurted out "You know, the Philippines..." and "Can I ...."

"Oh, sorry, you go first," he told her.

"Well, pardon me if I'm a little forward, but the Philippines is a lovely place, not like here on Pagasa. If you ever want to come visit, well, I would be happy to be your tour guide," she said in a rush, as if afraid she wouldn't get it all out.

He realized that he would like that.

"I don't know when I could," he said, seeing her eyes fall in disappointment before he hurriedly added, "but I would be happy to come visit. Maybe when this deployment is over next year."

She smiled in relief and moved closer to him as they turned their attention to the last of the Chinese to board the plane. He wondered if he should put his arm around her, but it didn't seem right. Too much had happened here. He would keep in contact, and if things worked out, he would give it a shot. Until then, he still had his platoon to lead.

Chapter 39
Beijing

Things moved quickly in the Chinese government. This was not like the West where things could drag out over years of indecision. General Chen looked at the document he was carrying. He folded it back up and slid it into his uniform jacket. He felt it was his duty to deliver it.

Had it only been 6 days, he wondered?

The PLA Chief of Staff had to admit that he had been more than tempted to choose a different path last week, when the fate of the nation rested solely on his shoulders. He could have sided with the general secretary, the man who had just two days ago turned in his resignation for "health reasons." He could have given General Li what he needed to succeed, and the People's Republic might now be the premier power in the world. But at what cost? The Americans held that unenviable position at the moment, and look what it has done to their economy. They still spent more on defense than the rest of the world combined.

And he had been tempted to do what the members of the Politburo likely feared, to stage a coup. As a military man, he held a degree of contempt for his seniors, those who made the decision for soldiers to follow but never once having worn a uniform. But that temptation was quickly squashed. He didn't want to become one of those whom he held in such low regard. And he knew he probably would be a poor leader. He knew the military, not agriculture, not diplomacy, not manufacturing and all the other things that made a country run.

In the end, despite his dislike of the politicians who wanted all of this to end, he knew what he had to do. He knew the Americans, NATO, and Russia feared the growing might of China, and they would not let this stand, especially the Americans. The cost to China would just be too high. Could they prevail? Possibly, but if they did, they would have destroyed their markets, the very people they needed to make China prosper.

The order to fire upon the *Jinggan Shan* had been perhaps the most difficult order he had ever given. Those were China's brave sons, men who were doing their patriotic duty. They had been blameless in everything.

But the ever increasingly aggressive American rhetoric required a dramatic action to assure the Americans that this was a mistake. That ended up being the party line, that this was all a tragic mistake instigated by others. This had been an action against both China and the US. Muslim terrorists, probably based in the southern Philippines, had hacked into Chinese systems and given the wrong information, leading the Chinese to believe that the US had planned the entire thing out and were in fact the aggressors. It had all been part of a plan to pit the two super powers against each other.

Aided by a few Chinese criminals in high places, out for financial gain, they had taken control of small number of Chinese assets, namely two ships. It had taken a particularly astute and dedicated PLA Air Force captain to uncover the truth.

Had the Americans bought the story? Most likely not. But they didn't want war, either, and this gave them an out. The sinking of the *Jinggan Shan* provided the "punishment" to China, as would the coming announcement at the UN that the People's Republic ceded any claims, now and in the future, to the Wanli Shitang.

Of course, there were the survivors of the force to be considered as well. The crew of the *Changbai Shan* had been fairly easy. They had never closed with the Americans nor the Taiwan Chinese. It was easy to give them the concocted account of events. For the soldiers and Marines on Thitu, however, this was a bit problematic. They had fought both the Filipinos and the Americans. To convince them that this was all a big mistake, that "terrorists" had created the situation, was a little more difficult, especially as the unit that had fired the Long Sword cruise missiles had neglected to remove the red star that showed to anyone who saw it whose missile it was. Without that, it could have been a terrorist missile that had sunk the ship. All the surviving soldiers and Marines had been transferred to a base in Xinjiang for "debriefing." General Chen was confident that the new version of events would in fact soon become the ground truth.

The Politburo had authorized payments for all the Filipinos killed, most of them being in the C-130 that had been shot down, and to rebuild their town on Thitu... that is, Pagasa Island. But that was peanuts compared to perhaps the biggest loss of this entire debacle, that the Americans now knew of the Chinese ability to hack and even shut down systems. The entire American military was now undergoing "routine maintenance," ferreting out every piece of equipment and every program where the Chinese had gained control. This was a huge loss, but as the largest exporter of military hardware, a loss that the Americans did not want to advertise that had happened. They would clean their own systems first, then slowly clean the systems of all their client states.

This loss was the reason why Sung Wenyan was still among the breathing. He was scum, to be sure, but scum with a talent. He would help the task force that would design new ways to hack the Americans and other nations. They had lost one avenue, so a new avenue would have to be built.

He reached the locked door, guarded by a lone soldier. The soldier snapped to attention, then turned to unlock the door. General Chen took off his cover and stepped inside.

General Li was sitting at the bare desk in the middle of the room, writing. A perfectly made bed was in back of him. At least his discipline hadn't faltered.

General Li looked up at his entrance, then stood, coming to attention and saluting.

General Chen said nothing, but took the paper out of his pocket and handed it to him. General Li read it, no change of expression coming over his face. That was about what Chen had expected.

The paper was a simple receipt—for one round of ammunition. It was made out to General Li's family. They owed the Chinese government five yuan, payable upon receipt.

General Li folded the paper and handed it back to the chief of staff.

"Thank you for being the one to let me know. Do I have time to finish the letter to my family?" he calmly asked as if nothing much was wrong.

"Yes, you have another hour or so. I will personally deliver any letters you write."

"And the others?"

"Senior Captain Chou has received the same sentence, as has Commander Hung. No decision has been made yet for Admiral Hung. Your command center staff has been sentenced to prison for various lengths of time, excepting Sung Wenyan."

That brought a rise to Li's eyebrows. "Sung Wenyan? But..." he paused until understanding dawned on him. "Ah, his unique skills are probably needed."

General Chen merely nodded.

"It is sad that someone like him will thrive, when the patriots receive a different future, or lack thereof, I should say."

This was the closest General Li would come to a complaint, General Chen knew.

"And...?" the question was left unsaid.

General Chen chose to respond to it. "The general secretary has decided to resign due to health concerns. The third-ranked vice deputy has also decided to resign. All signs point to Second-ranked Vice Premier Wang Jinping being appointed as the new general secretary."

"Ah, the general secretary? I wasn't sure if this all went that high."

"Yes, well, the ex-general secretary. I'll leave you now to finish your letters."

General Li saluted his chief of staff, who returned the salute and turned to leave. General Li's question stopped him, though.

"Why, General Chen? We could have succeeded."

General Chen hesitated. He could just walk out, his duty done. Li had chosen, and chosen wrong. Now he would pay the price for that failure.

Without turning around, he simply said, "China will succeed. But this was not the way to do it. The cost would have been too high. China is bigger than you, than me, than the Politburo. It will last much longer than any of us, which will be evident to you personally in about an hour."

With that, he knocked on the door, walking out after the guard opened it.

Ben dan, he thought as he started walking down the hallway.

Normally, when someone called someone else a dumb egg, it was with disdain. But this time, he used the term with a degree of sympathy. General Li was a good man. Good, but dumb. To think he could play politics with the masters was idiocy. He never should have assumed anything. Without direct, specific orders, he should never have planned even one move. He let his ego and nationalistic righteousness overcome common sense. As a general consequence, the nation had been harmed. As a personal consequence, his family received a bill for five yuan, the cost of one 7.62 mm round.

Chapter 40
Cebu, The Philippines

1st Lieutenant Peter Van Slyke watched the carousel, waiting for his bag to appear. He wasn't sure what to expect. He had arrived in Manila the evening before, and the frantic pace of that mega-metropolis had beaten him down. He had been told by others to take only the official airport taxis, but as he got to his hotel near the US embassy in Ermita, he had been astonished at the filth and poverty that surrounded the Best Western. Inside, though, the hotel had been much nicer, so he never left, eating in the hotel restaurant before trying to get some sleep.

He had gotten up early, then taken the hotel car back to the airport where he caught the 8:05 Cebu Pacific flight to Cebu. The flight was different, to say the least. At one point, all the flight attendants had broken out into song and dance.

The plane reached Cebu in an hour, and Pete took in the blue, blue ocean as it came in to land on the small island just off the main island of Cebu itself. The plane landed with barely a jar and quickly taxied to the terminal.

Things seemed much more laid back in Cebu, and he immediately felt at ease. The weather was pleasantly warm, but he wished he had worn shorts instead of his Levis which were sticking a bit. He was just happy to be out of his uniform. He knew his haircut labeled him as a Marine, as the Filipino ticket checker back in Manila had greeted him with a "semper fi," but with jeans and a polo shirt, he still felt the stress of the deployment slough away.

He had twelve more days of leave left to get rid of all the stress. He had visited Sgt McNamara back at the Wounded Warrior battalion on the first day of his post-deployment leave, marveling at how far he had come in his rehabilitation. The doctors gave the sergeant a good chance at a complete recovery. The second day of his leave had been taking the flight from San Diego to Manila. Now, his real leave was about to begin.

He had just spotted his seabag when he felt a light touch on his arm. He turned to see Analiza standing there, simply lovely in her white cotton blouse and tan shorts. He felt his heart miss a beat.

"Hi Peter, welcome to Cebu," she told him, her face radiant.

Pete didn't know what would come of his week-and-a-half in Cebu, but he was sure going to enjoy finding out.

Thank you for reading The Marines. I hope you enjoyed it. I would love to get your feedback, either in a review or through the website http://www.returnofthemarines.com.

The Return of the Marines

The Few

The Proud

The Marines

Other Books by Jonathan P. Brazee

To the Shores of Tripoli

Darwin's Quest: The Search for the Ultimate Survivor

Wererat

GLOSSARY

CMC	Central Military Commission
HE	High Explosive
HEAA	High Explosive Anti-Armor
HEDP	High Explosive Dual Purpose (warhead)
IAR	Infantry Automatic Rifle
LCAC	Landing Craft Air Cushion
LCpl	Lance Corporal
MCMAP	Marine Corps Martial Arts Program
MEU	Marine Expeditionary Unit
PCF	Private First Class
PLA	People's Liberation Army
ROC	Republic of China (Taiwan)
SIGINT	Signal Intelligence
SMAW	Shoulder-Launched Multipurpose Assault Weapon
SP	Shore Patrol
SRAW	Short-Range Assault Weapon
VA	Veterans Administration